The SOUND of FREEDOM

ANN MURTAGH

THE O'BRIEN PRESS
DUBLIN

First published 2020 by The O'Brien Press Ltd,
12 Terenure Road East, Rathgar, Dublin 6, D06 HD27, Ireland.
Tel: +353 1 4923333; Fax: +353 1 4922777
E-mail: books@obrien.ie
Website: www.obrien.ie
The O'Brien Press is a member of Publishing Ireland.

ISBN: 978-1-78849-125-9

7 6 5 4 3 2 1
24 23 22 21 20

Printed and bound by Norhaven Paperback A/S, Denmark.
The paper in this book is produced using pulp from managed forests.

The Sound of Freedom receives financial assistance from the Arts Council

Published in:

The SOUND of FREEDOM

ANN MURTAGH spent her first seven years in the Bronx, New York. After a short time in Dublin, her family moved to Kells, Co. Meath. She qualified as a primary teacher and later received an MA in Local History from NUI Maynooth. A member of both Meath Archaeological and Historical Society and Kilkenny Archaeological Society, she has given lectures to both groups. Ann has designed and facilitated history courses for teachers both locally and nationally. She has three sons, Daniel, Bill and Matt, and lives with her husband, Richard, and two dogs in Kilkenny City.

DEDICATION

To my sons, Daniel, Bill and Matt

ACKNOWLEDGEMENTS

I was inspired to write this book while working on a commission from Barnstorm Theatre Company to develop school resources for their play, *The Messenger*.

Thanks to Michael O'Brien and all at The O'Brien Press, especially my editor, Emer Ryan. I am indebted to other people along the way: my uncle and mentor, Oliver Nolan, for feedback on an early draft; my cousin Deirdre Murtagh, for proofreading and comments; my sons Bill and Matt, for sharing their perspectives on the story; my son Daniel and his wife Lindsay, for their steadfast support from the start. My mother Christina Murtagh's local knowledge of the Collinstown area proved to be invaluable. Sheena Wilkinson, Sarah Webb, and the staff and pupils of Kilkenny School Project all played a role in making the manuscript worthy of publication.

Finally, my gratitude and love to my husband, Richard White, for believing I could do it and never being shy of saying it.

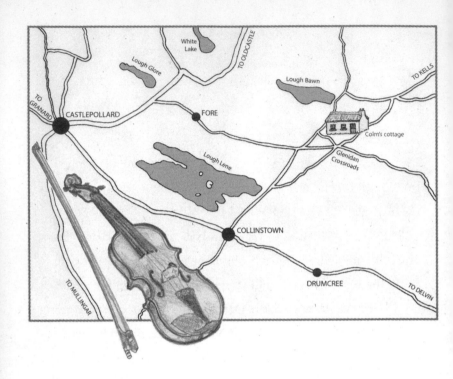

Chapter One

I marched off the road to the tune in my head.

'Soldiers are we, whose lives are pledged to Ireland, some have—'

A hand sprang out, grabbed my arm and dragged me into the cottage.

'Stop here,' a man's voice said. 'It's not safe above.'

The latch clicked as the door closed. I pulled free and stumbled into the dark kitchen, landing on the flagstones beside Jip, the old black and white sheepdog. Reeking of damp fur, he leaned over and licked my face.

'Tom Cooke, for God's sake, be careful!' said Mrs Friary towards the shadows inside the door. She turned to me and whispered, 'They're above with your father.'

Tom slid from the door over to the window. His brown moustache twitched as he peeped through the curtains.

'They're up there this twenty minutes,' he said. 'Spotted them driving up the boreen when I was crossing into the Fort Field.'

'And Nan?' I asked, unfastening the school bag on my back.

'Castlepollard,' said Mrs Friary. 'Gone this two hours. At least she's been spared the sight of them.'

7

'What are they after?' I asked.

'Anything that gives local Sinn Féiners a bad name, especially if they're stirring things up, like your father,' said Tom. 'We're all under instructions from Dev not to have anything to do with the RIC and it's not sitting well with them.'

'Dev, did you say?' said Mrs Friary plunging her hand into a basin of water on the table. 'I'll not have the President of the Dáil's name shortened in *this* house. He's Mr de Valera here.'

She plucked a dishcloth out of the water and started wringing it.

'Begging your pardon, *Mr de Valera*,' said Tom, sounding very posh. He had worked in London before the war and had a good ear for accents.

'Those peelers were beyond in Delvin last Tuesday in Francie Briody's,' said Mrs Friary, ignoring him. 'And by the time the search was over, there wasn't a stick of furniture standing.' Mrs Friary and Nan always called the police the 'peelers'. When I asked Dad why, he said Robert Peel, a prime minister in England, came up with the idea of policemen in the first place.

'Not a stick of furniture!' Mrs Friary had said. No wonder people were calling the Royal Irish Constabulary 'the enemy'. Now the enemy had come to our house. What would they do to my violin, lying in its shiny black case behind the good chair in the parlour? All day in school I'd been thinking of the tunes I'd play, like 'MacDermott's Hornpipe' and 'The Morning Dew'. Now, in the hands of the enemy, my fiddle could be a pile of broken strings and wood … unless I got up there in time.

'Thanks for the warning, but I'm not staying,' I said.

'What do you mean not staying? Are you out of your mind?' asked Mrs Friary. She blocked my way, a wet dishcloth held in one fist.

'No, I'm *using* my mind. They might stop if I walk in on them.'

'It's too risky,' said Tom from the window, pushing his head to the corner to get the best view of the boreen. 'I've stayed here with good reason. If I went up, and your father and I both got arrested, who'd look after the place then? Wait until they've left and then we'll head up.'

'You're talking good sense there, Tom,' said Mrs Friary, as she wiped specks of dough from the oilcloth on the table. Jip watched my every move, his tail brushing the floor. *He* knew I couldn't trust those policemen around my fiddle. I counted to three in my head, leapt over him, grabbed my school bag and bolted out the door. I was scurrying up the lane towards our house before anyone could shout 'Up the Republic!'

I ran along the ridge of grass in the middle, trying not to slip into the tracks of muck each side. Once I passed the Fort Field, I slowed down, threw my school bag on my back and walked into the yard. The RIC had arrived in a Crossley Tender. They must have pulled up and got out in a hurry; the door on the driver's side was open, nearly touching the post of the garden gate.

'Didn't you know that RIC stands for Royal Irish Chariot?' Tom Cooke had joked once. After that, we always called Crossley Tenders 'chariots'.

As I passed the woodshed, Roddy, our sheepdog, whimpered. The rare sound of any motor always sent him into a frenzy of barking. I could imagine the rumpus he caused for our so-called visitors! And now here he was, locked up like a criminal.

'Shh, Roddy,' I whispered. 'I'll let you out when they're gone.'

I squelched along the muddy path between the chariot and the hedge, avoiding the pile of fresh horse dung that the RIC had driven through and spread. Through the windows of the chariot, I watched a hen scratch for worms beside the open door of the house. This was the right time for me to walk across and in, bag on my back, coming home from school. I would have done that *if* I hadn't seen the greatcoat thrown over the back of the driver's seat and a folded sheet of paper sticking out of the pocket.

If I was brave enough to take that paper, it would prove that I was ready to join the Volunteers. There could be some useful information in there too. Maybe a police file of some sort that the Volunteers would love to get their hands on. If I was right, I could be signed up by tomorrow, a couple of months ahead of my birthday. I could be drilling with the men in the fields by Sunday.

'When it's your fourteenth birthday, you and I will have a talk,' Dad had said that day in January, coming home from the fair in Castlepollard.

'A talk about what?' I begged him to tell me, but he didn't get to answer because of the four heifers we were droving home from the fair. A gate was left open at Lynch's in Anker-land and Dad had to run ahead to stand with his arms out, blocking the way. Behind him, a light shone from the work-shop in the yard and the cold air was filled with the clanging of Joe Lynch's hammer on the hoop of a barrel.

'Can't you give me a hint?' I said to Dad when he joined me again.

'I said when you're fourteen and I meant it.'

From the tone of his voice, it was clear that asking any more questions was a waste of time. It was as if he put 'the talk' into a secret box, locked it and wrote 'Fourteenth Birthday' on it. But that didn't stop me thinking about it, and the more I thought about it, the more convinced I was that he was going to tell me I could join the Volunteers at last.

There was talk going on beyond in the house now. I took

the school bag off my back and threw it down at the gate. Leaning over the driver's seat, I slipped my hand into the pocket and pulled out the sheet of paper. My fingers felt something else. When my hand came out, it was holding a policeman's whistle. What would the lads say if they heard I'd got my hands on this? I put the paper and the whistle into my bag.

The voices coming from the kitchen were getting louder. I took a deep breath and was about to cross the yard, but stopped. Supposing the policemen came out and missed the paper and whistle? The first thing they'd do is search my school bag. Best get rid of it before I went near the house. It would only take a minute to find a hiding place in the garden. I thought of the old wooden butter box. Dry inside, and close to the gate, it couldn't be handier.

Crash! Someone smashed a chair or stool on the flagstone floor. I tried to take a step, but my legs were like lumps of wood rooted to the ground. My heart flipped and my mouth went dry.

'Cat got your tongue?' a voice roared.

Roddy started barking madly. He gave me such a start, I dropped the bag and darted into the garden, almost tripping over the butter box. Tom was right. Strolling into the kitchen in the hopes of stopping the RIC *was* too risky. I made my way through the scutch grass to the old holly tree in the hedge.

Here was a place to shelter until it was safe enough to creep back and grab my bag.

As I stared at the house through the gaps in the branches, I was thankful to be behind its prickly leaves. They were my shield from 'the long arm of the law'. What that long arm had done to Dad, my fiddle and the house, I could only imagine. But at that moment, it was a relief to be safely out of its reach.

Chapter Two

'You needn't play the silent man with me,' shouted one policeman. 'We know you've been a Rainbow Chaser for years.'

Sinn Féin members and supporters were well used to being called by the nickname 'Rainbow Chasers'.

'Oh yes! You'd be surprised at what we know,' said a man with a Dublin accent. 'What about your good friend Seán MacDermott? We know you met him here *and* in Galway.' Could this be the dreaded Kilcoyne?

'It's a wonder you weren't above in Dublin yourself — with all the *rebels,*' said the first voice. He said 'rebels' as if he was about to vomit. 'And you were spotted in Granard last year with Michael Collins.' Dad with Michael Collins — the Minister for Finance in the Dáil! This was news to me.

'Better start talking, Conneely!' This was definitely Kilcoyne. His voice was that loud, they'd have heard it below in Friary's. 'We need answers. We need them *now*. If you've any sense, you'll talk…. Tell us about Joe Kennedy and the meetings in Castlepollard.'

No answer. Something was thrown at a wall and crashed. It sounded like glass smashing or the delph from the dresser.

What were they doing to Dad?

'We know he's in the IRB.'

Dad still didn't say anything. There was another crash. I covered my ears.

'Who else is in it?'

Dad mumbled something.

Another crash. I held out very little hope for my fiddle now.

'Get out, ya lyin' Fenian!' bellowed Kilcoyne. Dad was flung out into the yard, falling onto his hands and knees in the gravel and mud. His cap fell off and his hair, mostly black but with strands of grey, was shorter than it looked this morning. Nan must have got after him with her scissors. He was no sooner down in the dirt than he was up, rubbing his hands on his trousers, blood dripping from a cut on his chin.

'Bad cess to you!' he said in Irish, and I echoed that curse at Kilcoyne. The Dubliner had arrived in Castlepollard in November, after soldiering for two years in the trenches. A true 'king and country' man, he was the scourge of every Sinn Féiner for miles around. What right had he to throw my father out of his own home and into the muck?

Kilcoyne's dark green uniform filled the doorway before he lunged forward, holding up a small book. He swiped Dad on the back of the head with it.

'Are you in the army?' He stood behind Dad, who was a head taller than him.

'No,' said Dad.

'No, *sir*,' said Kilcoyne.

'No, sir,' mimicked Dad.

'Then what are you doing with an army book?' Kilcoyne marched in front of Dad and waved the book at him, almost slapping his face.

Dad stood, staring at the woodshed. His brown eyes hardly blinked.

'For a man fluent in both English and Irish, you haven't much to say for yourself, have you?'

Dad kept staring at the woodshed.

'You'll hear more about this, Conneely, and you'd better have mastered the power of speech by the next time we meet.'

He turned around and marched across the yard while Dad made his way into the house, only to be elbowed aside by a second policeman rushing out. I watched him make his way to the front of the chariot, but I didn't recognise him. He seemed to be waiting for Kilcoyne to get into the driver's seat before he turned the crank to start up the engine. Roddy was barking and jumping so wildly that the door of the woodshed vibrated. Kilcoyne stuffed the book into his jacket pocket. He walked around the back of the chariot, avoiding the dung, and was moving towards the driver's seat when he stumbled and fell in the mud near the garden gate.

'What the—?' he roared.

I leaned forward a few inches to see what had happened. The other policeman rushed over to him. He kicked something out of the way. It was my school bag.

'Are you all right?'

Kilcoyne stood up, waving away the hand that was held out to help him.

'Ugh!' He made a face at the dirt on his hands. 'Would you mind handing me out my coat, please?'

The greatcoat was pulled out and handed over. Kilcoyne plunged a hand into one of the pockets. Was that the pocket I'd gone through? I glanced around the garden. There was a gap in the hedge into the Fort Field if I needed to escape.

'Ah, here we are,' he said. When his hand came out, it clutched a big white hankie. He threw the coat back into the chariot and rubbed his hands first, then patted his trousers.

The other man picked up my bag. 'Looks like a school bag,' he said, holding it up by the strap.

'Wasn't there earlier,' said Kilcoyne. 'Might be the son's.'

Both men scanned the yard. Kilcoyne stared at the holly tree. Had he spotted me through the branches? I stood still. I didn't even blink. My mouth was so dry, I couldn't swallow, and that started an itch in my throat. The policemen opened the door of Dad's workshop. Trying my best not to give away my hiding place, I stuffed the damp woolly sleeve of my jumper into my mouth and closed my eyes, sinking to the ground. But nothing worked. I had to cough, a raspy splutter of a cough. Roddy's barking became so frantic, I reckoned he had heard me and was howling to be let out.

'Shut up, you cursed mongrel!' shouted Kilcoyne, kicking the door of the woodshed. Roddy snarled and I pictured him there in the darkness with his black furry coat, his teeth bared, ready to attack. Steps were coming towards the garden. As I crouched in the wet grass, I closed my eyes. A noise behind me made me jump. I opened my eyes, expecting to see Kilcoyne, waving the school bag at my face, the same way he had waved the book at Dad. But there was no policeman; only my school bag, pitched across the wall into the garden, landing among the drills of potatoes.

'Hardly worth wasting our time over a school bag,' said Kilcoyne. A door of the chariot slammed. Someone turned the hand crank to start the engine. That set Roddy off again. After the second door banged, the chariot spluttered, turned around in the yard and took off down the boreen. I grabbed my bag and tried to steady my knees to take steps through the garden gate into the yard. Dad stood at the door, hands by his sides in two fists.

I opened the shed door and a streak of black crossed the yard as Roddy bounded over to Dad and lay down in front of him. Dad patted him on the head, keeping his eyes on the boreen.

'The sooner that lot are out of our country, the better,' he said in Irish.

'Are you all right?' I asked.

He turned his eyes away from the boreen. The blood from his chin dripped onto his jumper.

'Bruised ... sore. But I'll heal. They've made a pig's dinner of the kitchen. It'll go hard on your Nan to see the state of it.'

'What about the rest of the house?'

Dad pulled out a hankie from his pocket and held it up to his chin.

'They got what they came for in the kitchen. They didn't go any further.'

The enemy hadn't gone into the parlour; my fiddle was safe! This called for a happy jig to be played in my head. I had to stop myself from laughing when I remembered one called 'The Angry Peeler'. I scratched Roddy's ear — the one with a little patch of white on it — as the tune took off.

'Better get the clean-up started before Nan gets home,' said Dad. 'And you should get out of those damp clothes or we might witness a rampage worse than any RIC raid.'

Roddy tried to follow us in, but Dad blocked him at the door.

'Stay, Roddy,' he said to the dog in English. He continued to me in Irish: 'He'll go after that jam that's all over the floor and it's not safe with the glass from the broken jars.'

'Why do you always speak English to Roddy?' I asked as I walked in ahead of him.

'Because English is good enough for dogs,' he said, closing the door behind him.

Chapter Three

'Just putting my school bag in here,' I called as I turned left inside the front door to the parlour. There, behind the good chair, was my violin case, exactly as I had left it. I dropped my school bag beside it and, pulling my damp jumper over my head, threw it on top.

Seconds later, I stood in the kitchen among broken glass and delph and sticky gooseberry jam thrown all over the floor. One of the three-legged stools was smashed in bits off the wall near the hearth. No wonder Dad didn't want to let Roddy in. He had Nan's rag bag and was pulling some rags out of it. I took up the bucket from the hearth.

'What about that book they found?' I asked, picking up bits of broken dinner plates and throwing them into the bucket. When I was little, I used to love looking at the Chinese men and women painted on those plates.

'Weren't they pulling the place asunder to get something on me and found it in the press behind Nan's jars of jam,' said Dad, wiping up the gooseberry jam from the flagstones with a rag. 'I got it from Terence McKay's cousin, a private in the army. Little gem of a book, the tips it gave me for training the Volunteers.'

'You never told me that you met Michael Collins,' I said.

'With good reason. Idle talk could get him into trouble.'

'And I heard Kilcoyne asking about the IRB,' I said.

'Yes…' said Dad, stopping to dab the cut on his chin with his hankie.

'What's that?'

'The Irish Republican Brotherhood.'

'Is that something new?' I asked.

'New? Not at all. It's been around these fifty-odd years.'

'That long? I can't believe I never heard of it.'

'You know Mam's favourite book in the parlour?'

'*Knocknagow?*'

'The man who wrote it—'

'Charles Kickham?'

'Well, he was head of the IRB back in the 1870s. And Seán and the men who organised the rebellion above in Dublin a few years ago — they were all in the IRB.'

'How is it I never heard of it?'

Dad paused and stared at the fire as if there was an answer burning in the hearth.

'Because the members meet in secret.'

'Why?'

'They want to end British rule in Ireland and set up a republic. And…'

He pulled another rag out of the rag bag and spoke very softly.

'They believe the only way to do that is through a rebellion.'

Dad picked up the besom and started sweeping the broken pieces of jam jars onto the shovel. I watched him and thought about the nights he wasn't home. It wasn't all Volunteer and Sinn Féin business. I wondered where did they meet? Who else was in it?

'Is Michael Collins in it?' I asked.

'No more talk about Michael Collins,' said Dad, dumping the pieces of broken glass into the bucket. I knew I wouldn't get any farther with that, so I ventured down another road with my questions.

'What age do you have to be to join the IRB?' I asked.

'Well over fourteen,' said Dad. 'It's a very serious step to take and not everyone is allowed in. You have to be proposed and seconded by men who are already members. Then you have to be prepared to take an oath.'

'I'll probably be in the Volunteers first?' I watched his face carefully as I said this.

'You will, all in good time,' he said, keeping his eyes on the shovel.

'Was my grandfather in the IRB?'

'Both your grandads were in it.'

'And what about Mam? Was she in Cumann na mBan?'

'No. The women hadn't anything like that back then. If she were alive today, she'd be a member, surely.'

I watched him sweeping up the broken glass. The firelight reflected on his sallow skin. Here was a man who was in the IRB, Sinn Féin and the Volunteers. And my mother would be in Cumann na mBan, if she were alive. Now it was time for me to do my bit for Ireland. It wasn't enough to speak Irish and play the fiddle anymore; now I wanted to learn fighting skills. I remembered Joe Kennedy's words at a Sinn Féin rally before the election in December: 'Music and language are good for the soul, but you have to be prepared to take action if you want results.'

Roddy started barking and running around the yard.

'There's Nan, now,' said Dad, as a bike flew past the window and disappeared into the woodshed. Seconds later, laden down with brown-papered parcels, she picked her steps around the puddles in the yard.

Mrs Friary must have warned her. The usual greeting in Irish called from the door never came. Instead, her head appeared around the partition, her lips in a straight line. A few strands of hair, once red, now white, had escaped from the tight bun she always wore. Her woollen cap smelled of damp wool and incense from the church. Treading through the smashed blue crockery, she paused in the middle of the floor. She surveyed the kitchen through her little round glasses. Her pale blue eyes blinked as she took everything in.

Nobody spoke. There wasn't even a crackle from the fire as

it waited to hear what she had to say about the damage. Only the clock on the mantelpiece was brave enough to tick. She glanced over the floor and the dresser but took closer note of the shelf over the hearth. The tin canisters with the faded poppies on them were as she had left them. On the far side of the clock, her Lipton's tea caddy and her old prayer book had not been touched; nor had the little red globe glowing under the picture of the Sacred Heart.

'I see they've spared the Sacred Heart lamp. They're not complete heathens, it would seem.'

'And the wedding photograph,' said Dad, pointing to the framed picture on the back wall. 'It'd kill me if that was damaged. It's Colm's favourite picture of his mother.'

Delia, my mother, stared at me from the picture, a younger version of Dad sitting beside her. All told, we had five photographs of her, the last one taken a few months before she died. At six years of age, I had declared that the wedding picture was my favourite and I'd been held to it ever since.

'What about yourself? I see you've collected another battle scar,' she said, looking at Dad's chin.

'Oh, it'll heal,' he said, kicking bits of the broken stool out of the way.

'That's only fit for kindling,' said Nan. 'Let's get back to work, lads. You've made a fair start.'

I threw the pieces of wood into the turf basket. And with

Nan shouting instructions like a sergeant in the army, we swept and cleaned the flagstones back to their bare glory. She even sprinkled holy water over the floor.

'That'll undo the villainy that was done to it,' she said.

Once I saw Nan lifting the bucket to fill the kettle, I slipped out of the kitchen. That sheet of paper drew me to the parlour like a pickpocket to a purse. I opened my school bag and took it out carefully. Moving over to the window, I unfolded it and read the words, printed by a typewriter.

Number and Name: No. 29 Seán Conneely

Address: Glenidan, Collinstown, Co. Westmeath, Native of Lettermore, Co. Galway

Occupation: Carpenter and Farmer

Membership: Captain of the Glenidan Irish Volunteers, Sinn Féin Gaelic Athletic Association, Gaelic League, Irish Republican Brotherhood

Prison Record: 1904: 3 months in Mountjoy for distributing leaflets condemning British Rule in Ireland.

1916: 6 months in Reading Gaol for being a member of an illegal organisation following the rebellion in Dublin.

1918: 3 months in Mountjoy for illegally collecting for Sinn Féin before the general election.

Family Background: Inherited present property from his wife who died in 1907. Lives at that address with his mother and son. His two brothers were active in the IRB before they left Galway for Portland, Maine, USA, in 1910.

Associates: Was an associate of Seán MacDermott, one of the leaders of the Dublin Rebellion (later executed). In the company of Michael Collins in Granard on 10 May 1918.

Close associate of Joseph Kennedy, Castlepollard.

Post of note since January 1918: Has received two letters from his brothers in Portland and one from a sister in New York City.

Dad would surely find this useful. It would give him a good idea of what the RIC had on him.

I noted the letter from his sister in the USA. That must be from Auntie Sheila. She and Nan had had a big falling out years ago when Nan was still living in Galway. That was before she moved to Glenidan to mind me when Mam died. An odd letter to Dad came from Sheila over the years, but she had never been to visit us.

'Colm!' Dad called from the kitchen. 'The tea is wet.'

'Coming,' I answered, folding the paper, placing it between the pages of one of my mother's books called *A Christmas*

Carol, and slotting the book in among the others on the parlour shelf. I had it all planned. Once Nan was in bed, I'd take it out and show it to him. Instead of waiting for my birthday, that talk could be over and done by midnight.

Chapter Four

As we pulled our chairs in to the table, we could all feel the bareness of the dresser's first two shelves. Kilcoyne had pulled his baton along two rows of plates, toppling them onto the flagstones. There were a few missing jars of gooseberry jam from the press and one less stool. The others were unaware that the house had two additions following the visit: the police file and the whistle.

I ate the last slice of Nan's railway cake and pushed the plate into the middle of the table. Dad hopped up and moved the china cat down from its place on the top shelf to the shelf below. Its painted face stared back at us blankly.

'That'll take the bare look off it.'

'Thank God my china cat wasn't touched by the enemy,' I said fervently.

Dad and Nan laughed. There was a standing joke in our house about the china cat, a souvenir bought by my Uncle Kit on a holiday in Bray. Kit was Mam's brother, and Dad was always joking that it had been left to me.

'*Constable* Kilcoyne knows quality when he sees it,' said Dad.

'Will you ever forget the roars of him today? "For a man

fluent in both English and Irish, you haven't much to say for yourself, have you?"' I said, imitating Kilcoyne's Dublin accent.

'Stop! You sound just like him,' said Dad, laughing.

'Never mind Kilcoyne. Can you take out your fiddle and play us a few tunes?' said Nan. 'God knows, we could do with a bit of cheering up this evening.'

I stepped into the parlour to get my fiddle, and in the quietness of the kitchen, raised it onto my shoulder. Resting my chin on it, I breathed in the smell of the wood as I tuned it. I started off with 'MacDermott's Hornpipe' and 'The Mullingar Races', two tunes that always got the toes tapping. I followed these with one of my favourite melodies: 'The South Wind'. After all, that was the tune that got me my new fiddle. I had played it after a Sinn Féin meeting in Castlepollard a year ago, on my old fiddle.

'Will you go and buy that lad a decent instrument?' I overheard Joe Kennedy say to Dad when I had finished. Three weeks later, my new fiddle landed on the kitchen table the morning of my thirteenth birthday. I thanked Dad for it, but always believed it was a gift from Joe Kennedy.

As 'The South Wind' filled the kitchen, a breeze whined outside through the branches at the back of the house. By the time the clock chimed ten, not only was the wind up, but the rain was lashing against the windowpanes. Nan hadn't gone to bed yet and Dad sat in his chair by the fire, his long legs stretched across in front of the hearth. His head had fallen to one side, his eyes closed. The cut on his chin was jagged and sore-looking.

'Seán,' said Nan, rapping his knee. He jumped up with a start and reached to wind the clock on the mantelpiece. As he stumbled towards the parlour to go down to his own room, he yawned 'goodnight'. I was about to follow him, but showing him the police file when he was this tired would be foolish. It would have to wait until morning. Nan raked the fire and put out the oil lamp. In the weak light of the embers, I pulled out the settle bed and eased my way into it for the night.

I covered my head with the blankets, but they were no match for the howl of the wind. And that RIC file! The words seemed to have marched off the paper and into my brain. To make matters worse, I could hear Kilcoyne's voice in my head: 'Some blackguard stole my information on Number 29!'

I peeped out and there he stood in front of the hearth, a jar of Nan's gooseberry jam in each hand. He swung his arm around and threw one of the jars at the back wall of the kitchen. The smash made me move further under the blankets. 'And someone stole my whistle,' he roared, hurling a second jar. When I peeped out again, I could see blobs of jam clinging to the wall for a few seconds, then sliding towards the floor. He leaned over and whispered, 'You're the boy who cares more about your violin than your father!'

'No!' I shouted, trying to shove him back. His chest felt hard. I pressed both hands on it and pushed and pushed. He stood still, even though I was using every ounce of power in my body. It was like trying to move the Hill of Ben. My hands were getting sore, and the harder I pushed, the taller he seemed to become. Taller, blockier, until I found my hands were pushing the side of the kitchen dresser.

Awake again, I climbed back into my settle bed. Outside, the wind still pounded the walls and roof of the cottage. It howled down the chimney like a chorus of devils screaming in agony. The flames leapt and crackled. On a shelf on its own, the china cat stared down at me with its painted face and whiskers, an evil curl on its lips. The oilcloth on the kitchen table quivered in the draughty corner, glowing with a ghostly sheen.

It was on a stormy night like this that my uncle Kit had died.

'The storm raged outside and the poor fella took to singing his head off in the bed. He sang every hymn known to man,' Mrs Friary, who was with him at the time, told me. 'It's the raving that comes with a fever.'

I asked where my mother was when this was going on.

'Your mother was living in Galway with your Dad and yourself. After her brother Kit died, she came back to her home place and of course brought the pair of you with her.'

There was something banging outside; it was getting louder. I closed my eyes and that Dickens story about Jacob Marley and other spirits who walked among their fellow men came into my head. I was sure the likes of it could happen. All things considered, I'd rather be tucked up safe in my settle bed than up and about like Scrooge was when Marley first came upon him. I moved down in my bed as far as I could go, my eyes tightly closed, and pulled the blankets up over my head. A blast of wind rattled the window and more banging followed.

That could be Uncle Kit's way of telling me that he's coming to visit, I thought. He had been a drummer in the Glenidan Fife and Drum Band.

'Kit Fitzsimons was the best drummer in five parishes,' the men in the band said. 'That's where you get your talent.'

His bass drum sat silently in the parlour beside the good chair. Nan had draped one of her black shawls over it out of respect for the 'poor dead gossan'. I often wondered if he was mad at me for leaving it to gather dust in the parlour while I played away on my fiddle instead. I opened my eyes again.

I was aware of a small light coming into the kitchen, but I dared not turn around. The light came closer. A voice spoke.

'I've left two letters on the table.' I pulled myself up in the settle bed.

'Dad?'

He put the candle down on the table.

'When you're in Castlepollard, will you post them before you go up to the hall?'

'Where are you going?' I asked.

'I'm off to get the Dublin train from Float Station,' Dad answered as he put his arm into the sleeve of his grey tweed coat. 'I heard they're watching Oldcastle.'

'I need to talk to you about something,' I said.

'Tell me tomorrow when I get back. I'm away out the door this minute,' he said, slapping his cap on. 'There'll be trees on the road after last night.'

Chapter Five

I was soon to find out how right Dad was. Branches lobbed off the elm trees covered the road towards Lough Bawn, six dead jackdaws scattered among them. Around the next bend, I was within inches of crashing into a limb of Daly's oak tree that hadn't quite broken off but was very close to it. But there was no getting past the old beech tree at Tom Cooke's house. It stretched across the road like a giant corpse covered in ivy. I had to go another way.

By the time I got to Castlepollard, I was dizzy from weaving in and out through broken branches. I got down off my bike and pushed it along Chapel Street. A couple of men were heading into the blacksmith's up ahead and I could hear Paddy Burke's hammer striking the anvil. Being able to hear the sounds of the forge at this distance wasn't a good sign; more rain was on its way.

A group of women huddled outside Gibney's Bar and Hardware, comparing notes on the damage done by the storm. I cycled past them into the yard strewn with twigs and leaves and wheeled my bike into one of the sheds. The church bell rang eleven o'clock as I hurried across the square with the letters. Everything was running late today. I was late for the first post and I was late for music. But I still had to wait my turn at the post office as two people were ahead of me.

I took my place behind an old man whose hand rested on a silver-mounted walking stick. Ahead of him stood a girl. I took a step sideways to see who it was. She was about my own height and wore a red woollen cap with a white tassel. Her thick black hair was woven into the longest plait I had ever seen, tied with a red ribbon at the end. It must be somebody visiting. She nudged a parcel across the counter towards Mrs Dobbs, the postmistress, who picked it up, adjusted her glasses and peered at the address.

'Belfast? That'll be ninepence, please.'

The girl put her money on the counter. Mrs Dobbs pounced on the coins, checked them quickly and dropped them into the till. A bony finger wagged over the first line of the address as if she were scolding the parcel.

'The postman in Belfast will have his work cut out for him trying to make out *that* name,' she said, shaking her head.

'It's in Irish,' said the girl. She had a Northern accent. I recognised it from a couple of men from Maghera who had used our place as a safe house in the past.

'I don't know why it couldn't be written in the King's English.'

The girl pointed to the parcel.

'Only the wee name's in Irish. The address is clearly written in English, so I don't see what the problem is.'

Mrs Dobbs's cheeks turned red. She tossed the parcel to one side, glaring at the girl.

'The problem is that we have to put up with little upstarts from Belfast who think they know it all.'

'Indeed, I don't know it all,' said the girl, 'but this I do know: I have every right to use m'own language in m'own country.'

Mrs Dobbs stood with her mouth open. This was as entertaining as a film in the cinema.

Before leaving the counter, the girl turned back and said in Irish, 'Will you give over with your gapin' at me as if I brought a plague on your poxy post office!'

It was Ulster Irish, rarely heard in Westmeath. We spoke Connaught Irish at home and I found the northern dialect difficult to understand. But I loved the way she broadened the 'a' sound and I loved her spirit. It made me want to cheer. If I did, though, that old crow behind the counter mightn't serve me, so I said nothing. The girl from Belfast turned around. Cheeks as red as her cap and a scowl that would turn milk sour, she marched out.

'Did you ever see the likes, Mr Mulrooney?' said Mrs Dobbs to the man with the walking stick. She leaned forward. 'I blame Sinn Féin for the likes of that impertinence. A bunch of nobodies pretending they're somebodies.'

'Who is she?' asked Mr Mulrooney.

'She appeared out of nowhere last Monday and is staying with the Maguires over in Drumcree — herself and a younger brother, I believe.

'Those Maguires are Shinners?' Mr Mulrooney asked. 'I must say, I'm surprised. The old man was a "Home Ruler". I remember he canvassed for the Irish Party in the old days.'

'The old man was, but the present crowd? Rainbow Chasers every last one of them. Did you not hear Pat Maguire spent a couple of weeks in jail for collecting for Sinn Féin before the election?' Mrs Dobbs leaned over, put her elbow on the counter and lowered her voice. 'Speaking of jail, I don't mind telling you that the parcel that young madam was posting was addressed to Crumlin Road Jail in Belfast.'

I coughed, not an ordinary cough, but one of those throaty 'Excuse me, I'm here, you know' coughs. As much as I was interested in hearing about the girl from Belfast, I had letters to post. *She* certainly wouldn't wait around until Mrs Dobbs was ready to serve her and, by gum, neither would I. My cough worked like a full stop. Mr Mulrooney cleared his throat, asked for three stamps, paid for them and walked smartly past me. I stepped forward to the counter and was met by Mrs Dobbs's hostile eyes.

'Yes?'

'Two stamps … *más é do thoil é.*' I put my money out.

She paused, her lips making an even thinner line, then tore off two stamps and slapped them onto the counter. The door of the post office opened. Somebody came in behind me.

'*Go raibh maith agat,*' I said as I swiped the stamps and stuck them onto the letters.

'That's what I love to hear,' said a voice. 'The bit of Irish being spoken.'

I turned around. It was Mrs Friary with a grin on her face that clearly said she wasn't mad at me for running out of her house.

Mrs Dobbs scowled and tried to summon some smart words to her mouth, but none came. I wished the girl from Belfast had been there to see how a few words in Irish put the old biddy in her place.

'*Slán leat,*' said Mrs Friary, smiling as I passed her.

'*Slán agat,*' I said, as I tossed the letters into the postbox and swaggered out the door.

A dozen boys and girls waited outside the Commercial Hall for music. With trees and branches down on every road, the Gaelic League class for adults had started late and still wasn't over. I joined my friend, Peter Quinn. He started telling me about the old oak tree that had fallen on their farm, but my ears picked up a voice among the girls beside us.

'Excuse me, is this the hall for the music lessons?'

It was the girl from Belfast. Her voice went up the scale towards a high point at the end of the question. It was like listening to a new tune on the fiddle.

'It is,' answered Maisie, Peter's sister. 'You're joining us?'

'Aye, I am,' she said. 'Alice. Alice McCluskey.' I glanced sideways without making it obvious to Peter. Alice held out her hand to Maisie. Some of the other girls crowded in to meet the new girl, too.

The door opened and men and women, poured out, all speaking Irish. I knew most of the men from the Volunteers and two or three of the women from calling to Nan for cures.

Inside, the hall smelled of damp coats. There were four rows of chairs in front of the stage.

'She's definitely not from here,' whispered Peter, as Alice's red woollen cap bounced past us.

Maisie steered Alice towards the front row to join the other girls. Peter and I sat with the boys at the back.

'Who's the new girl?' asked Bill Matthews, joining us.

'She's from Belfast,' I told them both. We rarely met anyone from further away than Mullingar, so Belfast was very exotic indeed. The three of us watched Alice sit down.

'Do you think she'll be coming to our school?' asked Peter.

'Don't think so,' I said. 'She's living over in Drumcree.'

'How do you know so much about her?' asked Bill who was standing with his mouth half-open; he couldn't move his eyes away.

'Oh, I make it my business to know these things,' I said. I didn't see the need to explain *how* I came to know them. And I thanked my lucky stars that I had the good fortune to overhear the conversation less than twenty minutes earlier in the post office.

Chapter Six

'Where's Mr McSorley?' Bill asked. 'It's not like him to be this late.'

Peter ran over to the door.

'No sign of him,' he called.

'Someone will have to step in for him,' shouted another of the boys at the back of the hall.

'You'll have to take over, *Master* Conneely,' said Bill.

One of the boys gave me a dig in the ribs. I was known for being a good mimic. Dad said it was my musical ear, but I also watched people carefully: how they stood, walked or held themselves when they spoke. Mr McSorley was one of my specialities.

'Go on, Conneely,' shouted another voice. The girls stopped talking and turned around. Alice raised herself slightly to see what was going on. She had taken her cap off. I jumped up and ran to the door to make sure there was still no sign of the music teacher. Peter closed the door and I came back up through the hall, exaggerating my steps from side to side the way Mr McSorley walked, and stood in front of the stage with my arms folded.

'You surely mean "Master *McSorley*", young Quinn,' I said

in Irish, making my voice sound as close to Mr McSorley's nasal tone as possible. 'Good morning, boys and girls. As well as practising your music, I hope you're all speaking Irish at home. At this stage, I would expect each and every one of you to know all of your prayers and salutations.'

Although Mr McSorley was our music teacher, he sometimes taught Irish for the Gaelic League and encouraged us to use it during class. I rubbed the end of my nose like he did when he got enthusiastic about what he was saying. I also copied the way he squinted over his glasses to look around at all the boys and girls. There were squeals of laughter from the girls. For the benefit of those who hadn't good Irish, I switched to English.

'No one can accuse us of being shoneens in the patriotic town of Castlepollard. Our people are alive with the Gaelic spirit. We've no time for those English music hall songs or those foreign foxtrots and the likes. We sing Irish songs. We play Irish music. We dance Irish dances. We speak Irish and an Irish version of English.'

I held out an imaginary sheet of paper and pushed an imaginary pair of glasses further up my nose.

'Let me see what we have on for today,' I said. 'Ah yes, "Brian Ború's March". But we need to warm up to play this magnificent tune. So, to rouse our Irish blood this morning, I suggest that the ladies all remove their ... themselves from their seats. Come on! Out ye come and line up in an orderly fashion.'

Mr McSorley regularly started class this way. I stood with one hand on my hip and the other beckoning the girls out. I often thought Mr McSorley looked like a policeman I saw in Mullingar, directing traffic. Peter snorted one of his big laughs. The girls paused. Who was going to go first?

'What about the boys?' shouted Maisie.

'Thank you for asking that question, Miss Quinn, but I'll be asking the gentlemen to fall in behind the fair ladies. Miss Quinn, will you lead the ladies out, please?' Maisie moved out into the middle of the floor and six other girls lined up behind her, including Alice. Only one girl, Molly McGrath, remained sitting.

'You're not joining us, Miss McGrath?' I asked in my best McSorley voice.

'I am not. I think it's sinful to be imitating the Master like that. I'll have nothing to do with it,' she said.

'For heaven's sake, Molly,' said Bill, who was her cousin. 'You know quite well, we all have great time for the Master. Sure, we're only having a bit of fun.'

'There is no obligation on you, Miss McGrath,' I continued in teacher voice. 'I'll be happy to have you sit this one out. Now, gentlemen,' I said, ushering out the boys with my hand. They lined up behind the girls.

'Let us march around the hall singing "Óró sé do bheatha bhaile", a song you're all familiar with. I will assume the position of leader.'

I walked to the top of the line, in front of the girls, moving my shoulders the way Mr McSorley always did. This brought on another chorus of laughs.

I grabbed a ruler that someone had left on a chair and held it up.

'One, two, three…'

We all started marching around the hall, singing. By the time we got to the second verse, I called a halt, holding up the ruler to do so, as Mr McSorley often did when he was pulling us up about something. This happened regularly. Praise from him came as rare as hens' teeth.

'The way you sang the last line in the chorus puts me in mind of a withered dandelion. Spirit is called for, boys and girls. Spirit!'

We all started again and this time sang the last line with gusto. After the third verse, I marched up the stairs onto the stage and was about to lead the troupe across when the door of the hall banged and a voice shouted.

'Excuse me!'

I stopped. The girls and boys behind me stopped. We all turned around. Peter and I looked at each other when we saw who it was.

A boy of sixteen marched up the hall, past Molly McGrath who was still sitting down. He was wearing a smart-looking tweed jacket and a flat cap. Once he reached the stage, he turned around and whipped his cap off, making sure we saw his fair hair slicked back with hair oil.

'I'm surprised at you, making game of your teacher and of the Irish language,' he said. Everyone stood still. I'm sure others who knew him from school, like me, thought that he was hardly the person to take us to task for bad behaviour.

'We were only having a bit of fun, Terence,' I said.

'Harmless fun, Terence,' echoed Peter.

Terence McKay lifted his head as if he had to remind us how far above us he had risen.

'I've been sent over to tell you that Mr McSorley is unable to take your lesson today. His house was badly damaged in the storm.' This was greeted with groans, followed by the boys and girls climbing down off the stage to pick up their instruments.

'Colm Conneely — a word please.'

He spoke the way an adult does to a child. I didn't answer. Alice made her way out with Maisie. Peter took his fiddle and his jacket. I nodded to let him know that it was all right for him to go off with the others. I took my time walking across the hall to pick up my own fiddle. I put on my jacket and slowly walked out of the hall so that any talking between us would be out on the road.

As I was leaning back against the wall outside, Alice's black hair came into my mind and I played a reel in my head called 'The Black-Haired Lass'. That sweet music was cut off by the voice of Terence McKay. Manly and all as it was, he being sixteen years old now, I could still hear traces of the younger voice that had taunted me for almost two years in school.

'I'm surprised at you making a mockery of—' he started.

'You've had your say about that. What did you want to see me about?' I asked.

'It's a Volunteer message.'

I said nothing and kept my eyes on the muddy footpath. I felt tiny drops of rain on my face.

'Will you let your father know that the delivery is ready to be collected?'

A 'delivery' was the word used for guns or ammunition.

'I'll tell him when he gets home tomorrow,' I answered, wiping the rain from my cheek with my sleeve.

'You do that,' he said. He scowled and I walked away, ignoring the *slán leat* that was grunted after me.

Chapter Seven

'That's good news about the delivery,' said Dad, the following evening. 'I'll have to go over to Chris Quinn about that.' Chris was Peter's father.

The smell of paint filled the workshop. Dad, with his tongue out to one side, was on his knees painting a leg of a table. I knew that he'd be happy about the arms coming to the Volunteers. I also knew that this would be a good time to tell him about the police file.

'There's something else,' I said, holding the sheet of paper up. I'd been looking forward to this moment all day.

'What's that?' he asked.

'I took it from the chariot the other day,' I said. 'It was in a coat pocket on the driver's seat.' He stood up, wiped his hands on his apron and took the paper. His lips moved as he mumbled the words he was reading.

'They're onto me, for sure. Why didn't you give me this the other night?'

'You were falling asleep. I was going to show it to you yesterday morning, but you left early for the train.'

'Good job I went from Float Station,' he said. 'In future,

if you get your hands on something like this, give it to me straightaway.'

He read through it a second time. I watched his face, hoping that maybe he'd give me a big pat on the back this time, and tell me to report for Volunteer duty on Sunday evening. He read to the end.

'I'll hold onto it now,' he said as he folded the page. It disappeared into the pocket of his apron. My hopes of joining the Volunteers ahead of my birthday disappeared too, like puffs of smoke up a chimney.

'Thanks, Colm,' he said in the way he would have thanked me for handing him a copybook from school. Down on his knees again, he took up the paintbrush. I waited as he dipped it into the paint and worked in little brushstrokes on the wood. He might say something else, I thought — I hoped. But he continued with his painting as if I wasn't there. I made up my mind. If the police file wasn't going to work, I'd have to ask the question myself.

'That talk you said we'd have when I turn fourteen—' I began.

He stopped painting but kept his eyes on the leg of the table.

'Yes?'

'I thought we might have it sooner?'

'Not 'til you're finished school,' he said. He started painting again and I knew he was waiting for me to leave. Even if the police file was of no use to him, I thought he might at least say something about how brave I was to take it. But no, he even begrudged the few minutes it took from his painting to look at it.

'Why do I have to wait?'

'I've my own reasons,' he said without looking up. I wanted to give the precious table he was painting a good kick. I wanted to grab the sheet of paper back out of his pocket and tear it to shreds. Instead, I turned around to walk out.

'Wait,' he said.

I turned back. Had he changed his mind?

'Yes?' I asked.

'You can come over to Quinns' if you want.'

Not the ending I had hoped for, but better than moping around at home.

'And don't mention that police file to anyone,' he added. I felt relieved that I hadn't told Peter about it, although I had felt obliged to tell him about the whistle.

Black clouds had unloaded heavy showers all day, but now the sky was filled with mares' tails. Dad and I crossed the stile into McCormack's field. Grazing cattle stood and studied us as we traipsed through the wet grass. A frosty silence hung between us. The sound of the cuckoo didn't cheer me up, nor the moorhens on the Prussian Pool now swollen from all the rain, nor the swallows flitting around the ruin where a soldier once lived who had fought with the Prussian Army. It wasn't until we were passing by a small wood on Quinns' land called 'the plantation' that the thaw started. It came about by a question from Dad.

'I wonder if Chris was at the Gaelic League meeting in Delvin today?'

I took the olive branch that was being offered.

'Peter didn't say anything about it.'

'Well, you know Chris. He makes up his mind at the last minute. I'd be surprised if he didn't go when Fr O'Flanagan was coming to speak at it.'

Fr O'Flanagan, Vice-President of Sinn Féin, was much in demand as a speaker.

'What about Joe?' I asked.

'He was to speak at it *and* Larry Ginnell.'

Dad had campaigned for local man Larry Ginnell in the elections before Christmas. He had been elected for Sinn Féin.

'Where did they have it?'

'In Denis Hegarty's field.'

'Wasn't much of a day for an outing in a field. Why didn't they have it in the new hall?' I asked.

'That's where it was supposed to be, but the Gaelic League booked it without saying who the speaker was. Once the parish priest found out it was Fr O'Flanagan, the whole thing was off.'

'Why was that?'

'He's in Sinn Féin, of course! The parish priest is a Home Ruler. Remember he stood on the Irish Party platform during the elections.'

I didn't say anything to this. Dad could easily start ranting about Sinn Féin versus the Irish Party, and as much as I liked Sinn Féin, I wasn't in the mood for a big discussion about politics. My thoughts turned to Alice. Had she gone to the Gaelic League meeting? I wondered. Drumcree wasn't far from Delvin and from the way Dad described it, it was an event the Maguires wouldn't miss.

I opened the heavy gate into the yard. Dad disappeared into the kitchen and out came Peter Quinn with two hurls and a sliotar. Although it was almost dark, he was determined to squeeze the last few minutes' hurling out of the day.

'Go easy on me, Peter,' I said before we started. Peter laughed because I always said that whenever we had a puck around. His long arm swung the hurl and aimed the sliotar towards my right arm.

There was a good reason for going easy; no matter how hard I had tried, I couldn't improve at hurling. Dad had pucked around with me at home, Peter and the lads had played with me in school, but none of it brought on my game.

Back in Third Class, we used to play 'Roads versus Fields'. The boys who walked to school along the road were the 'Roads' and those who went by the fields were the 'Fields'. Without fail, Terence McKay, then in Fifth Class, would tease me for being picked last. When the game was going on, and I'd miss the ball — which happened many's the time — he was always ready with a snide comment or a nasty laugh. And the worst part was how easily he got others to join in.

In my memory, one game stands out. Peter passed to me, I swung my hurl about to belt the sliotar between the two jumpers that were goalposts — I really felt I could have done it — when Terence, in a sneaky little move, put out his foot and tripped me.

'You tripped me!' I shouted at him, getting up.

'Stop making things up. You're such a sore loser!' said Terence. Then he started a chant: 'Sore loser, sore loser!'

Peter was the only one who stood up for me.

'I saw what you did,' he said.

'Standing up for our little friend, are we?' said Terence.

I walked away. It was the last time I held a hurl in school.

Peter, on the other hand, was a natural at hurling. And when he wanted a puck about in the yard, he knew what I was like.

He scooped up the sliotar and gave it a belt in such a way

that it was easy to hit back.

'Have you made your mind up about the job in Gibney's?' he asked.

'Yes. I'm not taking it. I told Dad on Tuesday and he's still mad at me.'

When I said these words, I thought about the police file and how little Dad had made of it. Was it because he was still cross with me for not taking the job?

'Did you not tell him about Terence?' Terence worked as a barman in Gibney's.

'I did. He won't believe me. He thinks I'm exaggerating all the time.'

'By the way, what did Terence want at music yesterday morning?'

'To pass a message on to Dad about a delivery,' I answered.

'The step of him in the door and the way he spoke to us,' said Peter. 'He'd be the last person I'd want to work with. Do you remember that time he locked me in the classroom after school? I still have the mark on my arm where I fell against a nail on the wall.'

'I remember. Weren't you trying to climb up to a window?' I said.

'I was scared out of my wits that I was going to have to spend the night there. The worst of it was, nobody would believe me that Terence locked me in.'

We pucked the sliotar back and forth a few times.

'Remember that time when Dad was brought off after the rebellion?' I said. That happened three years ago. On my way home from school, I met soldiers bringing him away to the barracks. Terence came up behind me and whispered in my ear.

'They're taking your father away to be shot,' he said.

I believed him and cried and wailed on the side of the road. Terence made sure the whole school knew about that the following day. He even got the little children in the Babies' Class to run after me shouting 'Cry Baby'.

Peter nodded. He knew how cruel Terence could be.

'I always thought he was jealous of the way you could speak Irish. You were always going to be better than him,' he said.

'I'd have thought being so good at football and hurling would be enough for him,' I said. 'If I hear another person call him "the star of the GAA", I'll scream.

'Don't' forget how wonderful he is for signing up so many new Volunteers. It's hardly surprising that someone like him with all his pals in the GAA should manage to do that,' said Peter.

All that could be heard in the next few minutes was the sound of the sliotar flying back and forth between us.

'If you're not going for the apprentice barman, what are you going to do?' asked Peter.

'I'd love to teach the fiddle or work at something with

music. I've been thinking lately that I'd like to go to America. I've two uncles in Portland and an aunt in New York.'

'New York?'

'Yes, and the funny thing is I hardly know anything about her. Nan and herself fell out years ago. I think Dad has her address. I have to let him get over not taking the job in Gibney's before I say anything to him about America.'

'What about the Volunteers?' asked Peter.

'I'm still on for joining. But if I go to America, I could work for the cause over there.'

'You could, indeed.'

I missed the sliotar and ran over towards the shed to scoop it up.

'What about you?' I asked.

'I'm going to...'

'Yes?'

'Can you keep a secret?'

'You know I can.'

'A letter came from Mam's uncle in Argentina, this week. He wants me to come out and work for him.'

'That's some letter to get. Are you going to go?'

'Mam and Dad want me to go. He has no children and he's looking to leave his ranch to me.'

'A ranch, no less! You'd be mad not to go. By gum, I'll have to start calling you a gaucho.' We both laughed.

'Don't call me anything until it's all settled,' said Peter.

A rectangle of light stretched across the yard from the house as the kitchen door opened. Maisie called us in for a cup of tea. We walked towards the scullery door.

'About that whistle you took,' whispered Peter before we went inside. 'What are you going to do with it?'

'Scare the daylights out of some of the lads with it.'

'Good idea! And if I were you, I wouldn't be shy about telling how you got it. I bet that new girl would be impressed if she heard it.'

As I walked into the kitchen, I imagined myself telling the story to Alice and how at the end she would say the brave and daring deed it was — the very words I hadn't heard from Dad.

Chapter Eight

In the kitchen, Maisie was setting the table with teacups, saucers and plates. A big fruitcake sat in the middle. The children crowded around the table, all eight of them. Dad and Chris Quinn were huddled together over the hearth, discussing the meeting in Delvin. Chris had cycled over to it and was giving an enthusiastic account of the day.

'Aren't you lucky you're an only child?' said Peter, trying to reach the plate of sliced cake. 'It must be great to have the place all to yourself,' he continued, grabbing a slice and taking a big bite.

'Stop that, Peter Quinn,' said his mother. 'You should be grateful that you have your brothers and sisters.' She stood behind me and patted my shoulder. 'I'm sure if your mother hadn't been taken to God, she'd have had other children.'

'I'm sure she would have,' I mumbled. I knew that Peter was joking, but little did he know how much I envied him coming from a big family. When I was younger, I used to cross over the fields to play with the Quinns, every chance I had. The fun we had, jumping in the hay shed and playing hide and seek in the haggard.

I remembered one Saturday morning the summer before.

Chris had cleared out one of the sheds and Maisie decided that it was the ideal place to hold our own feis. Oliver and Joe were the two youngest and they sang 'Dilín Ó Deamhas'. Patsy gave a recitation of his favourite poem, 'The Old Brown Horse', and said he liked it better than any of the Irish poems and he didn't care what Maisie said; it was the only one he was going to do. Peter sang the 'Spailpín Fánach'. Maisie commented that it would have been grand if he hadn't sung like a drake.

I was to play the fiddle for the dancing. Chrissie and Kathleen did a two-hand reel. Margaret did a slip jig. Maisie herself was the last act. Before she came out on the 'stage', I had to announce that she had arrived in Glenidan at enormous expense. Once all her brothers and sisters finished clapping, she skipped into the barn with a tea towel attached to her blouse like a sash. Several holy medals were pinned onto it, copying the way Irish dancers wore their medals at a feis. The medals bobbed up and down as she danced a reel. Needless to say, she declared herself the winner.

And it wasn't only the fun that I was jealous of. There was something about having a mother in the house to come home to. I couldn't put my finger on what exactly it was, but I knew it was missing in our house.

'You had us in stitches the other day when you were doing Mr McSorley,' said Maisie. 'You should be on the stage or in the pictures.'

'That reminds me,' said Peter. 'Did you hear they're showing *Knocknagow* in the cinema in Oldcastle tomorrow?'

'That's one of my favourite books,' said Maisie. 'I can't wait to see the film. Are you going to it, Colm?'

'No, but I saw it last summer in the Picture Palace in Navan,' I said. 'Dad was on a job over there and the family brought me to see it. There was a woman from Tipperary sitting in front of us and she drove us all mad shouting out where the different scenes were filmed.'

Dad drained his cup and put it back on the table.

'Time to go,' he said, and we left the warm bright kitchen. The voices inside faded as we made our way down through the yard. Dad held the gate open as I walked through.

'Chris will collect the revolvers in the morning and leave them in the workshop,' he said.

The revolvers were delivered and stored safely in the workshop down the yard, and Saturday came around again. I whistled 'I'll Tell me Ma' as I rode my bike in for music lessons. Blue skies and bright sunshine added extra sheen to the morning. I hopped off my bike in Gibney's yard and wheeled it into one of the sheds. Once my eyes got used to the darkness, I could see that somebody else was propping up a bike in the shed.

A head beneath a red cap with a white tassel gave a little bob. Alice McCluskey said 'hello'.

'Hello,' I said, trying to steady my hands on the handlebars of the bike. 'Are you going to music?'

She fixed her cap further back on her head.

'Aye and I hope we've a better teacher than last week,' she said. She stopped and laughed and I laughed too and asked her name so that she could ask me mine. She shook hands with me. I never shook hands with anyone my own age before, let alone a girl. There was a pause. I tried to think of something to say to keep the chat going.

'What's your little brother's name?'

'How do you know I've a wee brother?' she asked.

I switched to Irish.

'I overheard Mrs Dobbs in the post office telling a man in front of me.'

'The woman in the post office? Seeing she was so put out at the sight of Irish, I'm surprised she was able to talk at all! My wee brother's name is James, called after the great James Connolly.'

When I heard her name one of the leaders of the 1916 Rebellion, I was tempted to tell her that my father had been a friend of Seán MacDermott's. That would surely impress her. But something stopped me. I wanted her to enjoy the importance of her brother's name. It might look like I was showing off, trying to be one up on her.

'My Ma knew James Connolly in Belfast,' continued Alice. Seán MacDermott also lived in Belfast at one time, but I held my whisht.

'Wasn't James Connolly head of the Citizen Army in the Rebellion?' I asked.

'Aye, he was,' she said. 'And Ma had planned to come down to Dublin to fight with them.'

'Fight?' I said, laughing. Alice didn't join in.

'I don't know what you're laughing at. The only reason, she didn't fight was that she was pregnant with wee James.'

I could feel my face turn red, and *she* laughed. People normally didn't say 'pregnant' in that barefaced way, but used words like 'in the family way'. And her mother wanted to fight? Surely that couldn't be right.

We walked out into the yard, towards the entrance onto the street.

'What instrument do you play?' I asked. She produced a tin whistle out of her coat pocket like a magician whipping a rabbit out of a hat.

'Beware! The Gaelic League will be after you to teach the whistle and to practise their Irish on you,' I said.

'Ach, they'll hardly be looking to speak Ulster Irish,' she said.

'What brings you down here?' I asked.

'We're stopping with the Maguires in Drumcree at the minute. Then we'll be joining my Ma in New York.'

'So, you're on your way to becoming a Yank,' I said and she smiled.

We started to cross the Square. Already I had pictured the pair of us making a grand entrance into the hall, but a figure standing in the doorway of Gibney's pounced on me before I took another step.

'Good morning,' Terence said to Alice.

'Good morning,' she answered. I said nothing.

'I need a word with you, Colm,' he said. 'You'll have to go ahead without him, Miss.' Alice waved at me and walked on. I stopped.

'Yes?'

He dropped his voice to a whisper.

'Joe Kennedy wants to see you and he said it's urgent.'

Alice was moving further away. As much as I'd like to forget that I'd heard this message and follow her across the Square, I knew I had no choice. If Joe sent for me, it was to Joe I had to go.

'He said he'd see you over in the snug.'

Over at the Pollard Arms, the bar, as usual, smelled of stout and cigarettes. I pushed the door open into the snug, the little room used by the ladies to have a quiet drink. Joe's clean-shaven face peered at me over the *Midland Reporter*. 'Good man,' he said, folding up the newspaper. I've had a visit from Sergeant McCarthy.'

I sat down on one of the benches.

'That book of drill instructions belonging to the British Army found in your house—'

'Yes?' I said.

'It's been reported to Dublin Castle. The sergeant wants to let your father know that the RIC will be coming to take him in tomorrow night, and obviously it would be in his interest *not* to be at home.'

'That's decent of him to let us know,' I said.

'In fact, he advises your father to sleep somewhere else over the next couple of weeks.'

'I'll tell him all that when I get home from music.'

'Sorry to say, there'll be no music today. You'll have to leave straightaway. Your Dad will need time to sort himself out at home and to organise a safe house.'

So much for looking forward to the lesson. No music today and no Alice.

'One more thing. Will you give him this message from me?'

It was a white envelope with no address on it.

'I will,' I said, putting it into my pocket.

Chapter Nine

'Oh, for God's sake, that's all I need,' said Dad when I delivered the message. 'But to be fair to that old Kerryman, he's always been a good friend.'

He drummed his fingers on the workbench, his dark eyes fixed on the pile of sawdust on the floor. Dad would be leaving to stay in a safe house again. Nan and I were used to his coming and going.

'And Joe told me to give you this,' I said, handing Dad the white envelope. He tore it open and read the note.

'It's the handguns in the workshop,' he said. 'Joe thinks it's too risky to leave them there. The police will be watching out for me, so *you'll* have to move them. Joe has a plan to get them over to Drumcree tomorrow.'

He read through the note again.

'You're to go to second Mass in Collinstown. Leave the chapel during communion and go to the pony and trap out the back. Pat Maguire will meet you there and take the goods from you.'

Joe Kennedy had written me into the plan and Dad was talking to me as if I was one of the Volunteers. My fortune was finally changing.

'Will it be safe outside the chapel?' I asked.

'During Mass it will be. There'll be nobody about at that time. Eight revolvers will be in the trap.'

'In the usual place, under the seat on the left?'

'Yes. And there's something else you can take care of for me. I was trying to work out how to get this envelope to Pat over the weekend.' He pulled out the drawer in the old table by the wall and rummaged under the dockets. The envelope he pulled out was already sealed. 'Now that you're meeting Pat, you've solved the problem.'

He wrote a name on it with a pencil. It was the last name I expected to see.

'This is for Alice McCluskey?' I asked.

'Yes, she's a girl that's staying with the Maguires at the moment,' said Dad.

'I know. I met her in Castlepollard today,' I said.

'You met her?'

'Yes, she was in town for the music lesson in the hall.'

'At music? That's good because Malachy won't charge her a penny. Now listen carefully. It's important that she gets this. The Maguires can't be expected to foot all the bills for herself and the brother, so there's some money in the envelope. We promised her mother we'd take care of them.'

'She was telling me her mother's in New York.'

'That's right. A great woman for the cause. The father is still in Belfast. The poor lad is in prison. He got into trouble with the police during the strike there after Christmas and ended up doing time.'

'So, I give Pat the envelope and the revolvers?'

'That's right. Tell him we did our best with the money. Her mother wanted more, but that's all we can afford at the moment.'

The choir was singing the entrance hymn while I sat into a seat in the men's aisle in Collinstown church. Wedged between two stout farmers who threw off heat like an oven, I was sorry I'd worn my coat. During the consecration, my eyelids drooped, but the bell brought me back to where I was and what I was about.

Soon afterwards, I felt a nudge. The man beside me wanted to go up for communion and I was blocking his way. I hopped up. The church organ wheezed the first line of 'Panis Angelicus'. Instead of falling into line with the men shuffling towards the altar, I squeezed through the latecomers blocking the door of the men's aisle, standing with their caps in their hands and reeking of sweat, mothballs and shoe polish. I pushed the door open.

Once I saw that the way was clear, I ran, passing the front of the church, stopping at the line of ponies and traps tethered to the wall. Our pony, Gus, was the very last one. I climbed up on the step of the trap. There was no sign of Pat yet.

Two blobs of blue in the distance turned into two girls cycling from the village. At the entrance to the church grounds, they stepped off their bikes and wheeled them up the avenue towards the church. Mass was nearly over. Where could they be going at this time? I kept my back to them as I patted Gus's nose and waited for them to pass by. That wasn't to be, as the whirr of the wheels stopped behind me.

'Colm Conneely, are you here on your own?'

I turned around. The voice belonged to Pat Maguire's sister, Madge. Behind her was Alice McCluskey. She was wearing a dark blue woman's coat that was too big for her.

'I am,' I answered. Madge stared at me. She was a couple of years older than me and a member of Cumann na mBan.

'Where's Seán?' she asked.

'Couldn't come. Had to respond to an emergency,' I answered. 'Where's Pat?'

'He had to respond to an emergency too,' said Madge.

'Oh?' I said.

'He couldn't make this delivery, because he had a delivery of his own during the night. His wife had twin boys shortly after midnight.' A smile passed over the faces of the two girls.

'By gum, that *was* some emergency! Who's coming to collect the goods?'

'*We* are, of course,' said Madge. 'Alice here is staying with Pat, so he nominated her to work with me.' She glanced over at the church. 'We need to start moving fast.'

I looked at the bikes.

'Where are you going to put them?'

'We've specially designed pockets in our coats,' said Alice.

She was about to open her coat to show me, but the sound of a car engine on the road stopped her. We all froze.

'Where's it going?' asked Madge, not turning around.

'Turned off the road. Coming up towards the church,' I muttered. 'Make it look as if Alice has been taken ill.'

The girls flung their bicycles onto the ground. Madge helped Alice up into the trap. The two of them sat across from me, Madge rubbing Alice's back. I looked over at the car. A man sat behind the wheel. A woman beside him, in a navy felt hat, stared at us. Which way were they going to go? Left, and they would be beside us in seconds. Right would mean they were going up to the parochial house.

They paused and every second seemed like an hour. I glanced over. It looked like they were discussing something. The engine kept running as a car door opened. The woman in a navy tweed suit walked towards us at a brisk pace.

'Coming this way,' I whispered to the girls who sat with their backs to her.

Alice's face, pale at the best of times, now looked the colour of buttermilk. Madge kept her eyes down. I rubbed the sweat on my forehead away with my sleeve.

'Hello there,' said the woman. Her two front teeth stuck out and she spoke with a deep voice. 'Are you all right?' This was said to Alice.

'I'm—'

'You're ill, aren't you? Then it's a good job I came along, given I'm a nurse!' She pointed one white-gloved hand towards the car. 'That's why I asked Fr Nolan if I could pop over to check on you.'

She climbed up into the trap, whipped off her gloves and started feeling Alice's forehead.

'Where's Pat Maguire?' she whispered.

This was a question we weren't expecting. None of us answered for a few seconds.

'I'm his sister,' said Madge. 'He couldn't come.'

'And you're taking the goods?' she asked. Madge nodded.

'Listen carefully,' whispered the woman. 'I'm Lizzie Scarlett — a sister of Katie's.'

'Katie who works in the priests' house?' asked Madge.

'The very woman. I'm on my way to her now, but I've a message for you. Don't bring the guns to Maguires. The house is being watched. Bring them to Bartle Ivory's.'

'Who sent you?' asked Madge.

'Joe Kennedy. He knew I was coming to see Katie today.'

Lizzie asked Alice to stick out her tongue so that she could check it. As she examined it, she spoke again.

'He also told me that you were bringing the delivery, Colm.'

Joe was telling her about *me*! She remembered my name *and* she was saying all of this in front of Alice. She waved over at the car.

'Have to go.'

She scurried back and climbed into the car without looking back at us. The car took off towards the parochial house, the far side of the church. Once we heard the engine turn off, Madge checked her watch.

'Wait for a minute to let them get into the house.'

We sat in silence. Alice fixed her gaze on Gus.

'Right, let's go!' said Madge.

Both girls stood up. The top of the seat was on hinges and I lifted it up to take out the flour bag with the revolvers wrapped in it. They took four each and as soon as you could say 'Cumann na mBan' the guns had disappeared among the folds of their coats.

The girls climbed down and picked up their bicycles. I jumped down from the trap and put my hand on Alice's sleeve.

'I've a message for you, Alice.' I loved saying her name. I couldn't help smiling at her and she smiled back and blushed.

'Wait for me at the gate, Madge,' she called. 'I'll only be a minute.'

'Don't delay too long,' said Madge. 'Remember what Pat said to us about moving away quickly.'

Alice stood there in the big blue coat and red-and-white cap; her hands tight on the handlebars.

'You've a message for *me*?' she asked. She pushed the bike closer.

I whipped out the envelope and gave it to her. She held the envelope up.

'Will I open it now?' she asked me. Her face was beaming. She was probably expecting this money and was delighted to get it.

'That's up to you,' I told her. 'But better be quick.'

Still smiling, Alice tore open the top of the envelope. A quick peek inside, then a puzzled look at me. The smile disappeared. Alice pulled the money out and poked her fingers inside to see if there was anything else. The blushes on her face spread and she blinked her eyes as if there was dust in them. She turned her back to me and counted the notes.

'This is only half of what my mother asked for.'

I heard the same tone in her voice as she had used in the post office.

'My father said that's all they can give at the moment,' I whispered.

She cleared her throat, pocketed the envelope and started to wheel the bicycle towards the gate.

'Thank you,' she said as she was moving away.

'Goodbye, Alice,' I called. She kept going.

The two girls mounted their bikes and cycled back towards the village. If you didn't know any better, you'd have seen two harmless girls, out on their bikes for a spin on a Sunday morning.

I headed back into the church and jostled for a place among the men inside the door. I tried to concentrate on the end of Mass, but the only prayer in my heart was for Alice. Even the last hymn, one of my favourites, couldn't lift my spirits.

Faith of our Fathers, holy faith.
We will be true to thee 'til death.

Singing those words always made me feel like you'd be true to Ireland, as well as to God. Today, I couldn't feel that faith. I was haunted by the disappointment in Alice's eyes and by the fact that she hadn't even said goodbye.

Chapter Ten

It was a relief to all of us that the guns were moved and were delivered to the right house, but when it came to Alice and what happened in Collinstown, I couldn't make up my mind. Was she disappointed with the money or was she expecting something from me, like a note about wanting to meet her? Either way, I couldn't rest easy until I spoke to her at music. Six more days to the next lesson, and you could be sure that they'd crawl by as slowly as a funeral procession.

If that wasn't bad enough, back home it was all talk about the RIC coming to the house during the night. Dad went through the questions again.

'If they ask you where I am?' he said, as he sorted out some papers on the kitchen table.

'You're gone to Dublin,' I answered.

'If they ask you why?'

'We don't know,' I said.

'If they ask you when I'm coming back?'

'We don't know,' I said.

Nan sat at the table, her knitting in the window untouched.

'I'm sticking to Irish,' she said. 'This is my home and I'm not changing for the likes of those pups.'

'Rightly so, but that'll vex them,' said Dad. 'If they start pulling the place apart, get out. Go down to Mrs Friary. She's ready if needs be.'

'Where will you be?' I asked.

'You know, I think I'll take myself to the pictures in Oldcastle. I didn't get to see *Knocknagow* that time in Navan, and this is the last night.'

'Where will you stay?'

'Might stay with Benny in Springhall.' Going out the door he called back, 'Don't forget to put the bar on the door!'

The bar was stored in a space in the wall behind the door. We hadn't used it since the election last December. Dad headed off to the cinema to see *Knocknagow* and I decided to take out *Knocknagow* from the books on the shelf to read for a second time. Chapter one still made me laugh. A young man, new to the area, thought he was being attacked by gunfire when he heard the banging of the Knocknagow drum on Christmas morning. I imagined the booming sound of the big bass drum, like Uncle Kit's drum sitting beside me.

I also imagined my mother sitting in the parlour reading these pages when she was a young girl, maybe the same age as I was now, and laughing with her brother, Kit, about the goings-on. I imagined Dad in Charlie Fox's cinema in Oldcastle, watching the scene at the pictures.

That night, as I slept in my settle bed, all that imagining

worked its way into my dreams. I was sitting in the dark, watching a film in a cinema. I was on my own. The reels on the projector made a sound like a bicycle chain. On the screen, a subtitle read: 'Local people enjoy Sinn Féin rally.' The opening scene was in some town I didn't recognise, but who was carrying the Sinn Féin banner only Mr McSorley and Tom Cooke! Several men and women marched behind them, all wearing Sinn Féin badges and tricolour armbands.

Next came the Cumann na mBan women, walking in rows of four. The leader was out on her own in front, swinging her arms like a soldier. There was something familiar about the way she held herself. I looked again. Her dark hair, swept up under a Cumann na mBan cap made her look older — but it was unmistakably Alice.

'Over here!' I wanted to shout at her, but what was the point? This was all happening on a cinema screen. Crowds gathered on the footpaths both sides, among them faces from my music class, the Gaelic League, the local GAA, not to mention neighbours and schoolmates. They were all clapping and cheering and waving little flags.

Next came the Volunteers led by Dad. Terence McKay, in full uniform, was on the outside, his nose in the air. I watched the well-known faces file past until the last Volunteer came into view. Then I sat up and stared at the screen with my mouth open. This young man kept step, head held high, the flag over one shoulder. The subtitle read: 'Colm Conneely, Rainbow Chaser, proudly carries the Tricolour.' I started clapping — I couldn't help myself. I felt so proud and excited to see that I was in the Volunteers at last — though it seemed strange to be sitting in a cinema, watching myself!

The Volunteers were followed by a fife and drum band. As usual, the drums were first, but when it came to the man playing the bass drum, a face looked out at me — a face I had seen in a photo. I only noticed now — with his turned-up nose — how much he looked like my mother. It was Uncle Kit. He beat the drum, staring straight ahead until he turned his head sideways for a second and gave me a cheeky wink. Hardly had he done this, when a subtitle appeared on the screen:

'A cloud comes over the happy scene.'

The next picture opened with a line of policemen standing across the road, blocking the drummers. Two of them started to pull the bass drum from Kit. He clung onto it, but his slight build was no match for the pair of burly men. As they hauled the drum away, Kit ran after them, pounding the back of the second one with his fists. Another policeman came up behind him.

'Watch out!' I shouted, forgetting for a moment that it was all happening on a screen and I was powerless to help. In a matter of seconds, Uncle Kit was handcuffed and taken away. Then the subtitle appeared:

'His faithful friend won't let him go without a fight.'

And there was Roddy, jumping up and down. He must have been barking as his mouth kept opening and closing. The policeman tried, again and again, to kick him out of the way, but Roddy dodged his big boot every time. Suddenly the screen looked like it was melting. The film reels went silent. All I could hear was Roddy barking.

It was outside and I was back in the 'real world'.

As loud as Roddy's frantic barking was, it didn't drown out other sounds. An engine roared into the yard and stopped outside the kitchen window. Two doors banged. A man's voice spoke loudly and was answered loudly by another. A short silence was followed by *bmmp, bmmp, bmmp!* Somebody's fist pounded on the door. I climbed out of bed and pulled on my trousers. Nan came into the kitchen, took the candle on the table and lit it from the embers in the fire.

'Who's there?' I called out.

'Police,' shouted a voice. 'Open up!'

Nan, with her apron over her nightdress, handed me the candle to hold as she pulled her black shawl around her shoulders.

'Hurry up!' said the same voice outside.

Handing the candle back to Nan, I removed the bar and lifted the latch. Before I had the door fully open, Kilcoyne barged in. Another policeman followed — a taller, blockier man. He almost knocked Nan over, pushing past.

'Mother of God!' she said in Irish.

'I'll start with that room off the kitchen,' said Kilcoyne, pointing towards Nan's room. 'You try the others.'

He disappeared into Nan's room while the other policeman took off towards the parlour. Nan trotted after him, but he swung around before she crossed the threshold.

'Where do you think you're going? Stay here!' he said as if he was speaking to a dog.

'She's a right to move around in her own home,' I said.

'You'd better shut up or you'll be saying goodbye to your own home,' he shouted and turned to go into the parlour.

'He'd better not touch any of the good furniture,' Nan whispered to me. She hovered around the parlour door. I put my hand on the smooth surface of my violin case on the kitchen table. If the enemy got rough, I had it ready to grab before we ran down the boreen to Mrs Friary.

The tall policeman arrived back first. He leaned over my settle bed and his two big hands patted the mattress in several places. Nan caught my eye and threw her own eyes up to heaven.

Kilcoyne put his head in the door from Nan's room. 'No sign,' he said.

'I felt the bed down in the other room,' said the second policeman. 'Cold. Nobody slept in it tonight.'

Kilcoyne walked around the settle bed. He gave a bad-tempered kick to it and stood in front of Nan, his thick lips in a pout.

'Where's that no-good son of yours?' he growled. I repeated the question in Irish.

'She said her son is gone to Dublin,' I said, translating Nan's answer.

'Expect us to believe that?' said Kilcoyne. 'If you're with-holding information, we could bring you in.' I changed that to Irish. Nan didn't answer. She kept staring at him.

'You're well able to speak English, Mrs Conneely. And you'd better start if you know what's good for you,' he said, coming up close to Nan. She backed towards the parlour door keeping her mouth in a firm line.

He was right. Nan did speak English. Mind you, twelve years ago, she had arrived from Galway able to speak only Irish. Dad helped her with the basics in English, but thanks to Mrs Friary she became fluent.

'A fast learner, your Nan,' Mrs Friary often told me.

'Are you listening to me, you old biddy?' Kilcoyne shouted. He came forward again, prodding Nan on the shoulder. She fell back and pushed the parlour door open. He sprang in after her and banged the door behind him.

I moved to go in after them, but the tall policeman stepped in front of me. He looked down his nose and held one big flat hand up at my chest. There was no getting past the likes of this man.

'Not so fast,' he said, hardly opening his mouth. He had a curl on his lip that reminded me of a dog when it snarls.

Chapter Eleven

Where's your father, boy?' the policeman asked me.

'Dublin.'

'What train did he go on?' he asked. I remembered that the train station in Oldcastle was being watched.

'The half-five from Float Station.'

'Is that right?' he said. 'We had the half-five train from Float Station watched, and nobody fitting your father's description boarded it.'

I wasn't expecting that answer. My legs started to shake. I tried to steady them.

'Maybe he missed it?'

'Oh yes, and maybe he never went to Float Station in the first place?'

I didn't answer. Kilcoyne's shouting was getting louder from the parlour.

'Your son is well known to the police,' he roared. Nan shouted back in Irish that she wasn't telling him anything.

I felt my shirt being grabbed by the collar.

'Tell us where he is, you little cur!' the tall policeman said into my ear.

'He's gone to Dublin,' I said. I could smell whiskey off his breath.

He threw me onto the flagstones. My knees felt sore, but I jumped up as if it hadn't done anything to me. *Crash* came from the parlour. It was Uncle Kit's bass drum. Nan screamed.

'I didn't know it was a crime to go to Dublin,' I said.

'Hold your tongue!' he snapped. 'You'll be taken in tonight if you're not careful.'

His face came close to mine again and he raised his fist as if he was about to hit me. His arm trembled. He dropped it as soon as Kilcoyne blustered through from the parlour.

'Come on,' he said. 'We're wasting our time here.' He kicked a bucket of turf at the wall as he walked past. It tipped over, scattering sods and turf mould over the floor. They slammed the door behind them. Roddy started barking again as the truck's engine was cranked up. We could hear Jip joining in the chorus down at Friary's as the truck drove out of the yard.

I hurried to the parlour. Nan lay on the floor, clutching the black shawl, white hair all around her face as the pins holding her bun in place had all fallen out. Uncle Kit's drum lay beside her, the calf-skin head all torn. I had to get her up. Lying down was giving in to the enemy. I took her hand to help her.

'Did he hit you, Nan? Did he do anything to you?' I asked.

'He pushed me in here. I didn't know what he might do to me … but no, he didn't lay another hand on me,' she said. 'But with all that shouting and kicking things around, he might as well have been beating me.'

'The big bully! Barging in here and frightening an old woman out of her wits.'

'With all his huffing and puffing, he thought he would make me turn informer. But I stuck to the Irish and never told him where your father was,' she said. I picked up the shawl from the floor and handed it to her.

'And that was the best weapon you could have used. Dad'll be proud of you. Come on back to the kitchen and I'll make you a cup of tea.'

Nan's lip quivered as we walked past the broken drum. She tried not to cry, but the tears came in spite of her. Once her hanky was pulled out of her apron pocket, she took off her glasses and wiped her eyes. I couldn't help but notice her lined face and her tired eyes.

'Don't worry about that. I'll take care of it tomorrow,' I said. I shuddered as the image from my dream of Uncle Kit being led away came back to me.

'Ah, the poor dead gossan,' said Nan. 'I only met him once when your Mam and Dad got married. And to think of all I did to mind that drum.'

'I'm sorry to hear about your ordeal at the weekend,' said Mr McSorley at the end of music class the following Saturday. He had his sleeves rolled up. Summer had come with a vengeance, and the hall had become a hothouse by noon.

'Your poor Nan was in a state about Kit's old drum being kicked in,' he continued.

Almost a week had gone by since the RIC had been to our house. Nan was still a bit shaken but enjoyed the constant stream of visitors coming to the house to console her. At this moment, though, Alice was on my mind more than Nan. She hadn't shown up for music.

We all started packing our instruments away. Mr McSorley bobbed his head sideways, letting me know that he wanted to have a quiet word. No doubt it would be a message for Dad, probably something to do with the Volunteers. I walked up to him and he handed me a folded copy of *The Meath Chronicle*. It was left open at a page where one of the advertisements had a circle drawn around it.

'I was shown this at a Gaelic League meeting in Oldcastle last night,' said the music teacher, pushing his glasses up further on his nose. 'And the first person I thought of was you.'

I read the advertisement:

'They've fiddle first on the list!' I said. 'Would I have a chance at all, do you think?'

'Every chance, I'd say.' He gave me a friendly punch on the shoulder.

'Would it matter if I'm not fourteen yet?' I asked.

'Are you not almost fourteen? Sure, you're so close, I don't think it would make any difference. A couple of fiddle players in Oldcastle are applying for it — older lads, mind — but truth be told, they don't hold a candle to yourself.'

To think of all the times he pulled me up for missing a note or slipping up on the timing. Hearing those words from him put me at a loss as to what to say.

'Bring it home and show it to your Dad and Nan. If you're going ahead with it, I'll write a reference for you.'

I was walking out of the hall when he called after me.

'Don't you have two uncles over in the States?'

'Yes, and an aunt,' I said.

'Is that right? I thought it was only the two uncles,' said Mr McSorley. 'You might be able to meet up with them all if you go out there.'

As I walked out of the hall, I gave a skip and a jump to the 'Tailor's Thimble Reel', which was playing in my head. When Alice hadn't turned up at music, my heart had sunk like a stone in a bog hole. But that little advertisement in my pocket lightened my step. It filled my head with tunes I could play for the Yanks. If they wanted a hornpipe, 'The Green Fields of America' would be a great choice.

Back in Glenidan, I marched past the door of the house and down the yard to the workshop, where Dad was planing a piece of wood. He nodded at me and I waited until he'd finished.

'Mr McSorley gave me this today.' I handed him the page from the newspaper. He read through the advertisement.

'You're not over fourteen,' he said, handing it back to me.

'He said I was close enough that it shouldn't make a difference,' I argued.

'You don't have to be taking off to America to get a good start.' He began planing the wood again.

I kept going so he wouldn't start harping on about the job

in Gibney's. 'This is a great chance for me,' I said. 'There's no guarantee that I'll get it, but I'd like to have a go. Isn't that what your brothers did? They left when they got the chance of a job. And didn't your sister do the same?'

Dad stopped. His eyes were still on the wood.

'Which sister are you talking about?'

'What do you mean "which sister"? Don't you have only the one sister?' I asked.

'Oh, yes, Sheila,' Dad said.

'Think of it: two uncles and an aunt I've never met. I might be able to visit them if I get the job.'

He didn't say anything to this.

'So, can I write for an appointment?' I asked.

Dad kept his eyes on the floor and didn't speak. He shrugged his shoulders.

'All right. Go ahead,' he said. 'I'll never hear the end of it otherwise'. He picked up the plane and got back to work.

'Thanks,' I said and turned to walk out. At least he hadn't said 'no'.

'Let me handle Nan,' he called after me.

I had passed the water barrel at the end of the house when I remembered the newspaper was still in the workshop. Roddy followed me down the yard as I made my way back to get it. The door was still open. I stopped. There was a sound coming from the workshop.

I couldn't bring myself to walk in when I heard it. I crept around the back and, climbing up on a couple of old blocks, I peeped through the little window. There was Dad, slumped over the workbench, his head buried in his arm, sobbing. I ducked in case I was spotted. Dad — crying? The only time I had ever seen him cry was the day we heard Seán MacDermott was executed in Dublin. I thought about going in, but what could I say? He might be embarrassed. *I* definitely felt embarrassed so no doubt he'd be mortified if I walked in.

Best leave the newspaper there and come back later. I walked quietly past the door. Dad was blowing his nose. I wondered what could have upset him. As I walked back towards the house, I considered possible reasons, from Nan being unwell, to the death of someone he knew in Galway. But for each reason I came to the same conclusion: surely, he would have told me about it? I entered the kitchen, ill at ease and none the wiser.

Chapter Twelve

'There's a lot of unrest over in Delvin at the moment,' Dad said, putting the *Midland Reporter* down on the table the following day. 'It'll take the spotlight off me for a change. I think I'll chance staying at home for the next few nights.'

'Take note, Mrs Conneely,' said Mrs Friary who had come up looking for a knitting pattern. 'Colm's not the "man of the house" for the next few nights.'

Mrs Friary knew that once Nan started calling me by that name, she gave me loads of extra work. The two women were sitting at each end of the table, sipping cups of tea.

Roddy wandered into the kitchen, followed by Jip. The two dogs were panting, after playing around in the yard, and both lay down in the coolest place in the kitchen, under the back window. A statue of the Blessed Virgin Mary, with arms outstretched beneath a blue cloak, looked down on them from the window-sill — now our 'May Altar'.

Every May, Nan took the statue out of her bedroom and put it standing on a little white linen cloth with 'Ave Maria' embroidered on it in blue thread. A jar of fresh flowers stood either side of it. Today Nan had cut some white lilac in the garden. The fragrance filled the kitchen.

I sat at the table with the others, opened the newspaper to see what was on in the next few weeks and spotted the following advertisement:

COLLINSTOWN SPORTS

Running, Cycling, Swimming, Obstacle Races,

Ladies' Cycle Race, Boating Trips to

all or any part of the Islands,

Picnics and numerous other attractions

IS THE ORDER FOR

Sunday, 8 June. Starting: 3pm

AT

Lough Lene, Collinstown

Remember the date, and don't forget to inquire *at once* about boating and other facilities to secure an enjoyable evening for yourself and your friends!

'I see the sports day isn't banned by the RIC this year like some people were saying,' I said, showing the notice to Dad.

'It isn't banned, but you can be sure the place will be crawling with police,' said Dad.

'Especially as the GAA is running it,' said Nan. 'They know quite well that a lot of the Volunteers are GAA men.'

'Madge Maguire should enter the Ladies' Cycle Race,' said

Mrs Friary. 'I never saw a girl like her to pedal up a hill.'

'What about Alice McCluskey?' I said, trying to sound as casual as possible. 'She wasn't at music yesterday. Is she still in Maguires?'

'She is,' said Nan. 'I had to call over on Monday to Judith Maguire, with a cure for the boils. She said Alice is a great help with the twins.'

So, Alice was still with the Maguires. Would she still be with them come Sports Day in Collinstown?

'I hope you're still on for taking out the boat,' said Mrs Friary. 'That's my favourite part of Sports Day.'

We had a boat on Lough Lene that Uncle Kit had left us. Every year we rowed out to the islands to raise funds for the GAA.

'Well?' I asked Dad, thinking how great it would be to sit across from Alice in it.

'I'll hardly be around with all the police expected.'

'Where will you be?' I asked.

'Not sure yet.'

'Will I be in charge of it, then?'

'No, you're still a bit young.' He stood up.

'Have you someone in mind?'

'I might have,' he answered.

'Who?'

He slapped the tablecloth with the newspaper.

'I don't know. I'll find somebody. For God's sake, will you stop pestering me!' He tucked the newspaper under his arm. 'I'll be in the workshop,' he said to Nan.

'Ah don't be so hard on the gosson,' said Mrs Friary. 'He's only looking forward to the day out.'

'I know, I know,' said Dad. 'It's just I've so much to think about, the boat is the least of my concerns.' He left and Mrs Friary turned to me.

'Never mind him, Colm. He'll find someone. Sure as there's moss on the Furry Hill, it'll be sorted.'

Sorted by whom? I wondered. And why was I always passed? I marched out of the kitchen, across the yard towards the garden. My head was bursting with what I wanted to say. Sports Day in Collinstown was one of the best days of the year. It could even be the best day ever if Alice was there. She would love the boat and the lake and rowing to the islands.

I was in no humour for the stiffness of the garden gate, and I kicked it open, dotting the grass with specks of peeling white paint. I left it as it was; I couldn't care less what beast would pass through it and trample on the cabbages and potatoes.

'What did that poor gate ever do to you?' said a voice behind me. It was Tom Cooke. 'Is your Dad at home?'

'He's in the workshop. Tom, are you going to be around on Sports Day in Collinstown?'

'Maybe at the very end of it. Why do you ask?'

'I thought you might be able to take charge of the boat seeing as Dad has to lie low.'

'I've another job on that day, so I won't be able to do it.'

'What kind of job?'

'Can't tell you now but you'll hear about it in due course.'

'Me?'

'I have to talk to your father before I say anything.'

'Ah, come on, Tom. Don't half tell me things!'

'Stop — I'm not saying a word about it.

'But—'

'Not a word! This is worse than being questioned by the RIC!' He held both hands up. 'Have to go down to your Dad, now. No more questions!'

What was this mysterious job? Nobody was willing to answer any questions today. Dad and Tom asked questions all the time. When they wanted to check if a plan had a good chance of working, the questions flew all over the place. Why was it wrong for me to do the same?

I climbed onto the wall and swung up onto the horse chestnut tree that was growing in the field outside the garden. On a thick branch that felt like sitting on a big wooden shoulder, I lay back against the trunk.

As a little boy, I called the pink and yellow flowers of the chestnut 'candles'. From climbing the tree so often, I had always noticed the different stages of the candles, but today I was amazed to see my tree all lit up. It must have been weeks since I was up here. This is what happened when you were forced to be 'man of the house'. You didn't even have a minute to climb your favourite tree.

Chapter Thirteen

'Colm!'

Nan called me from the garden as I was crossing the yard. It was the last Tuesday in May and I was on my way home from school.

'There's a letter for you on the table.'

I dropped my school bag at the door. Inside, a white envelope with my name and address, complete with a Dublin postmark, lay on the flowery oilcloth. I grabbed it and tore it open.

> J.D. Pictures
> c/o Gresham Hotel
> O'Connell Street
> Dublin
> Friday, 23 May 1919

Dear Master Conneely,

Regarding your letter of application, please come to the Saint Vincent de Paul Hall in Kells, Co. Meath, at 11 o'clock on Saturday, 14 June. You will be asked to play two reels, a jig and a hornpipe, of your own choice.

Yours sincerely,

Mary Brown

I ran out to the garden. Nan was picking rhubarb.

'I've got an appointment on Saturday, fourteenth of June,' I said.

'Where?' She kept her head down.

'The new hall in Kells.'

'I suppose you'll wear your good jacket and tie,' she said.

'Of course, I will, and I've to choose some tunes, though I've a fair idea already of what I'm going to play,' I said, folding the sheet of paper and putting it back in the envelope.

She added more pink stalks of rhubarb to her basket.

'I can't believe that letter came. I was giving up hope of hearing back from them.'

Nan kept picking.

'I wonder if Dad will lend me his bike that day,' I said. My own bike wasn't fit for long journeys.

'I couldn't tell you,' she said.

She stood up and wiped her forehead.

'The job's in New York?' she asked.

'Yes — and other cities on the east coast of America.'

'I'd think long and hard about going to New York,' she said. 'It can be a cruel old place when things aren't working out for you.'

'Who told you that?' I asked.

'Relations of mine who have gone there over the years.'

'Who?' I wondered if she'd mention Auntie Sheila.

'My sisters, Peggy and Nancy, my brother, Andy, Lord have mercy on him, and my cousins, Bridgie and Maggie. If any of them had a chance of a good job in Ireland, they'd have never left.'

I knew where this was going.

'Why don't you change your mind and take that job in Gibney's?' she asked, putting her hands on her hips.

'I've explained why often enough. I'm not going to work there and that's that.'

She grabbed the handle of the basket of rhubarb, made that annoying clicking sound with her teeth, and took off towards the yard. I knew better than to go after her. If you disagreed with Nan, she always went into a huff and you might as well be talking to the garden gate if you thought you were going to change her mind.

Dad walked into the kitchen that evening. Nan was still at the milking.

'I've news,' I said.

'Indeed?'

'I'm to go to the new hall in Kells to play for the Americans,' I said.

'When?' he asked. I told him the date and the time.

'Well, that's that then,' he said, picking up the teapot and scalding it with boiling water. He emptied the water into a bucket.

'I've to pick my own tunes,' I said. He knew all the tunes I played.

'You'll have no problem with that,' he said, scooping some tea leaves into the teapot.

'What about your bike?' I asked.

'What about it?' he said, filling the teapot with water from the kettle.

'Could I borrow it?'

'I'll let you know closer to the day,' he said. 'I might be needing it.'

'What'll I do if you're using it?'

'You could always try Nan,' he said, pouring himself a cup of tea and adding milk and two spoons of sugar.

He put on his glasses, took the folded newspaper from the window-sill and spread it out on the table. I might as well have been the three-legged stool at the fire, for all the notice he was giving me.

'Why don't you want me to go?' I asked.

He took off his glasses.

'I don't want you to go to Kells because I don't want you to go to America.'

'Why not?'

'It's the timing of things. I'm going to be away from home more and more on Sinn Féin and Volunteers' business and the likes. You'll be needed here to stay with Nan.'

I thought about the day I'd seen him weeping in the workshop. Was that because he was worried about Nan being left on her own? But what about my dreams of going to America?

'So, I have to give up all my chances of going to America?'

'Have you no heart? She's getting older and it's not right for her to be on her own.'

'You could always ask Terence McKay to stay with her, seeing as he's so obliging and you think so much of him.'

'Terence?' He shook his head. 'What has Terence to do with it, for heaven's sake, Colm?'

He picked up the newspaper and started reading it.

I had to get out of the house. I headed for the pump in the yard and started pumping water, even though there wasn't a bucket in sight. The water poured into the trough which began to overflow. Roddy slipped in beside me and started lapping from the puddle around the trough. When he'd finished, I scratched his ear.

'You know what'd help now?' I said to him. Both his ears pricked up into triangles. 'You're right as usual. Music.'

He knew what I was saying, even though I spoke to him in Irish. I whistled 'God Save Ireland' and walked across the yard to the rhythm of it. In the parlour, I took out my fiddle.

Dad appeared at the door.

'I've got some news myself.'

'Yes?'

'It's about Sports Day,' he said. 'Terence McKay is going to do the boat rides.'

'Terence?'

I put down my fiddle.

'Is this a joke because of what I said about him minding Nan?'

'A joke? What are you talking about? Terence is ideal for the job.'

'Ideal for you, but not for me! Is there nobody else you could ask?'

'I couldn't pass him with all the work he's been doing for the Volunteers,' he said.

'Well, I'm not going if he's going,' I said.

Dad wasn't prepared to leave it at that.

'This isn't only about boat rides,' he said. 'It's for the GAA, and you know how many of them are in the Volunteers.'

He harped on and I only half-listened to him. Hadn't I heard it all before? He said something about the cause being bigger than our differences, on the need for Terence and myself to make our mark as the next generation, on our duty to Ireland.

'There's more to it than rowing the boat on the day. I've two jobs lined up for the pair of you. The Volunteers are involved

101

and they'll be keeping their eye on you as a possible new recruit, I can tell you.'

'Did Tom Cooke talk to you about one of the jobs?'

'He did.'

I sat down at the opposite side of the table.

'I'll go,' I said.

Chapter Fourteen

The prayers for fine weather for Sports Day were answered. Lough Lene stretched between the hills like a sheet of metal to walk over to the islands. Blue skies and sunshine were guaranteed to draw big crowds. Would they draw Alice? Moving through the racers, walkers, picnickers, jumpers and cyclists, I searched for her face. I even scoured the lake to see if she was among the swimmers.

There was nothing for it now but to climb into the boat opposite Terence. He was busy scanning the crowd to see who was about. His eyes rested on one spot and he shot up, rocking the boat and waving his arms.

'Ahoy, me hearties!'

Two red-haired boys sprinted towards the boat. The Reilly brothers were old classmates of Terence's. One after the other, they slapped Terence on the back, scrambled into the boat and dropped coins in my tin. One was wearing black trousers, the other brown; at least there was some way of telling them apart. Terence was about to push the boat out onto the lake when the twins' mother arrived with their little brother, Jimmy. As she tossed a coin into the tin, the expression on her face would stop any boat.

'Where are the pair of ye off to? I told you to bring Jimmy with you.'

'Ah, Mam, please—'

She lifted Jimmy into the boat.

'Sit in there between your brothers like a good lad,' she said sweetly. 'I'll see the pair of you later,' she hissed at the twins.

Terence picked up the oars and started rowing. Nobody spoke. Mrs Reilly stood on the lakeshore. Not until a comfortable distance stretched between the boat and the shore, was one word said.

'You'd better behave yourself, you little whinger,' said Brian.

'Leave me alone or I'll tell,' said Jimmy.

'Now, now, lads,' said Terence. 'We're out for an afternoon of enjoyment.'

The rhythm of the oars in the water lulled us all into a sleepy quietness.

'How's the fiddle-playing going?' Noel asked me after a few minutes.

Terence interrupted. 'Oh, the old string-scratching is going great, isn't it?'

'It is,' I answered. 'There's an *aeraíocht* in Castlepollard next month,' I said to Noel. 'I'll be string-scratching at that.'

The two boys laughed, but Terence frowned and kept a steady gaze ahead.

'What's an *aeraíocht*?' asked Jimmy.

'It's a big gathering of people that's held outside instead of inside. All sorts of things go on at it, like competitions for Irish music and dancing.'

'And some people say poems,' I added. 'Your brother won a medal last year for saying an Irish poem.'

'It's a great day out for grown-ups and children,' said Terence. 'That's why there's always a big crowd at an aeraíocht.'

'And because such big crowds come to aeraíochts, often an important person is invited to give a speech,' I said.

'Listen to the pair of you,' said Noel. 'Easily known that neither of you is saddled with an annoying little brother.'

'Do you know who they've invited to speak at *this* aeraíocht?' said Terence in a low voice, ignoring Noel's last comment.

'Éamon de Valera?' asked Noel.

'No, silly. Mrs Sheehy Skeffington. I heard Joe Kennedy and some of the lads arranging it,' said Terence.

'Who's she?' asked Noel.

'Don't you remember that man who was trying to stop looters during the rebellion in Dublin a few years ago?' asked Terence.

'Oh, yes,' said Brian. 'He was arrested by the British and shot a few days later.'

'That's the one,' said Terence. 'It's his widow that'll be making a speech.'

'Who was shot?' asked Jimmy, brightening up.

'A man in Dublin,' said Noel.

'I also heard Joe say that she was one of those women fighting for the vote. Six or seven years ago, when the vote wasn't given to women, she took to breaking windows in Dublin Castle, she was that fed up of waiting.'

'Who broke windows?' asked Jimmy.

'A woman in Dublin,' said Noel. 'Was she arrested?'

'She was and did time in prison. And the best thing is — she was a school teacher! Can you imagine Mrs Dunne hurling stones at the windows of Dublin Castle?'

We all laughed at this and the boat was a little unsteady for a time.

'Women have the vote now, so what's she going to speak about?' asked Noel.

'About Sinn Féin,' said Terence, putting on that annoying grown-up voice. 'She's in the Sinn Féin party now. The Volunteers are going to welcome her with a guard of honour.'

Jimmy tugged at Terence's sleeve.

'What's her name again?'

'Mrs Sheehy Skeffington,' said Terence.

I rowed and kept the rhythm of the 'Fisher's Hornpipe' in my head. We moored our boat beside three others in the little harbour at Nun's Island. Then we followed the path uphill through the trees, with Terence leading the way. Jimmy was finding it hard to keep up.

'Slow down,' he called.

'That's why we didn't want to bring you, you little twerp,' muttered Noel.

An old stone wall offered some shade from the sun. We dropped onto the mossy grass. Somewhere from the boggy ground near the shore, a snipe was calling 'chipper, chipper'.

'I need to go to the toilet,' said Jimmy.

'I'll take him,' said Noel. He jumped up and herded his brother around to the other side of the ruin.

Once they were out of sight, Terence spoke quietly.

'Brian, Colm and I have a job to do today.'

Brian sat up.

'What are you talking about?'

'Show him.'

I opened my kitbag and took out a furled-up flag. It was a tricolour.

'We've been asked to fly the flag today on Nun's Island,' I said.

'Couldn't we get arrested?' asked Brian.

'You'll be grand,' said Terence. 'If anyone lands in hot water, it'll be Colm and me.'

'Could you do something to distract Jimmy, while we're putting it up?' I asked Brian.

'What's around here?' said Brian. 'He likes climbing trees, but—'

Terence put his hand in his pocket.

'Look, here's an old ring I found in the yard behind Gibney's. Hide it somewhere and maybe you could convince him that it's treasure of some sort. Keep him busy for ten or fifteen minutes and we'll meet you back at the boat.'

Brian took the ring. As soon as the others arrived back, he spoke to his little brother.

'I'm off for a walk through the trees over there. I often heard that if you look carefully, you might be lucky enough to spot treasure.' He winked at Noel and bent down to the same level as Jimmy to talk to him. 'Would you like to go and have a look?'

'If we find any treasure, do I get to keep it?'

'Of course,' said Brian. He mouthed to Noel behind Jimmy's back: 'I'll explain.'

The three of them left and Terence turned to me.

'Let's get to work,' he said. We started on the path toward the crumbling walls up on the highest point. As we walked along, we could hear Noel talking to Jimmy.

'That ring belonged to a powerful woman who lived here

long ago. She was the most powerful woman in Ireland.'

'Is it a thousand years old?' asked Jimmy.

'I think it's two thousand,' said Noel.'

We followed the path through the trees that wound its way up to the old ruin. The quietness of that grassy patch surrounded by crumbling walls made you want to whisper. Maybe that's why there was no talk between us as we walked. Terence swung his arms like the men did when they were drilling with the Volunteers.

He stopped at what remained of the gable end of a little church. As he was the Volunteer, I handed him the flag. But he gave it back to me, saying, 'You climb up and I'll hand it up to you.'

I hesitated. Was he going to make me fall on purpose and spin it into a funny story to tell the twins when we got back?

'Why don't you go up?' I asked.

'It'll be easier for me to hand the flag up to you because I'm taller than you,' he said.

He cupped his hands to give me a leg up and I managed to get a foothold in the various hollow spaces in the old stone wall. If those nuns of long ago had set about leaving behind a good place to fly a flag, they couldn't have done a better job. The flagpole slipped easily between the crevices and, with some stones to make sure it stood in place, the flag fluttered in a breeze. Terence and I both saluted it before moving away quickly as Dad had instructed us to do.

Terence went ahead of me again as we scurried down the hill to the distant sound of cheers coming from the shore.

'Somebody's happy with us,' said Terence without turning around.

I didn't answer but walked proudly behind, avoiding a clump of nettles that grew close to the path. For the first time in years, I remembered what Terence was like before he was in Fifth Class. I remembered that he used to play with us younger lads sometimes and make us laugh. What made him change?

The twins were skimming stones on the lake while Jimmy, perched on a rock, counted every time a stone hit the water. I felt Terence's hand grip my arm.

'Before we join the others, are you fully informed about the second job today?'

'Of course, I am,' I said, pulling away from him.

'We've to meet Tom Cooke and Malachy McSorley at the bridge.'

'I'm aware of that,' I said. 'Once Dan Merriman comes to take over the boat, that's our signal to go.'

'To be honest, I wasn't in favour of involving a boy as young as you,' he said. 'I only agreed because we needed one to make the story look believable.'

'And I reckoned they must have been hard up for adults when I heard you were involved,' I said. He never turned around but his strides got longer and faster.

'Here are the others, so no more talk,' he said.

We climbed into the boat. Jimmy took out his ring and showed it to us.

'It's treasure and I'm going to keep it,' he whispered.

We took turns rowing back to the shore. Jimmy's eyelids drooped as he leaned against Noel. The rhythm of the rowing lulled him to sleep in minutes.

'How did you manage with the climbing?' Noel asked Terence.

'What do you mean?' asked Terence.

'Climbing up that old wall? You've got over your fear of heights?' asked Noel.

Terence pulled the oars and didn't answer straightaway.

'It made more sense for Colm to climb up and for me to hand it up to him,' he said tartly after a moment. 'I'm so much taller.'

I didn't say anything but plastered a smug grin on my face.

'Halloo boys!' a woman's voice called out from the shore. Jimmy woke up.

Mrs Reilly stood there, waving at Jimmy as if she had never left. The twins' red faces looked back towards the island as their little brother waved. We moored the boat, and Terence helped Jimmy to step out onto the shore. Our boat was among half a dozen that had been out to the islands.

'Next!' shouted Terence to the line of people behind the rope.

After all the searching earlier on, a pretty girl in a primrose yellow dress, her long black hair tied back with a black velvet ribbon was walking towards me.

'I see Nun's Island has decided to back the Republic,' said Alice, smiling. Madge came behind her in a light blue dress.

Alice held out her hand to be helped into the boat, but Terence grabbed it before I had a chance.

'Such a pleasure to welcome you aboard, Miss McCluskey,' he said, his voice dripping with charm.

'Thank you, my good man,' said Alice in a posh English accent.

'As for you, Miss Maguire—' Terence said to Madge. He didn't get to finish. A scream loud enough to be heard in Mullingar cut him short.

'My ring!' This was followed by screams of temper. The ring was under one of the seats in the boat. I grabbed it and held it up to Terence.

'Go on, quick!' he said.

I ran in the direction of the screams. Mrs Reilly was beside herself trying to get Jimmy to stop. The twins had already disappeared. A policeman arrived on the scene.

'Stop screaming, Jimmy, or that constable will arrest us,' she scolded.

Jimmy saw the policeman but kept on crying. He caught sight of me.

'Have you got my ring?' he said, his voice catching in his breath.

'I have,' I said, and put it into his hand.

Jimmy examined the ring. He held it tightly.

'You'd better not arrest us,' he said to the policeman, still half sobbing.

'Eh?' said the policeman.

'I have a ring belonging to the most powerful woman in Ireland,' shouted Jimmy.

'Oh,' said the policeman. 'Who would that be, then?' he asked, smiling at Mrs Reilly.

'Mrs Sheehy Skeffington! And if you arrest us, she'll break all the windows in the barracks.'

Chapter Fifteen

If I ran back fast enough, there might be time for another boat trip. But running through the crowd was like trying to sieve flour with a saucepan. The girls' under-eight race was about to begin and all the competitors were scrambling to get to the starting line. Calls for boys to line up for the egg-and-spoon race drew a horde of young lads into the mix, causing me to get more than one prod of a spoon in my back. Mothers and fathers shouted encouragement from the side or huddled in groups to catch up on the latest news. A man from the Gaelic League blocked me and started talking to me in Irish.

'No time, no time,' I said.

Mrs Friary's face beamed out at me from beneath her finest straw hat, as she made her way down to the boats.

'Isn't it a glorious day?' she said. 'I saw Dan Merriman climbing into your boat a few minutes ago, heading out on the lake with two girls. Couldn't see who they were. I'll head to Bill Matthews' boat further down.'

Dan Merriman was here already? Looking out on the lake, I could see that she was right. There he was, moving backwards and forwards as he pulled the oars of our boat. Alice and Madge, sitting opposite, both waved at me. I waved back and cursed under my breath. I hadn't even a chance to ask Alice if she was coming back to music.

'Missed the boat?' Maisie stood beside me and tittered. I stared at the yellow dress in the boat, fading away into the distance, the hoped-for afternoon disappearing with it. This was no cause for laughter.

'Did you see the flag that went up on the island earlier?' asked Maisie.

'I did,' I said.

'The police were in an awful flap about it,' she said. 'On my way over here, I heard a sergeant giving a couple of them a hard time. "Put up under our noses," he kept shouting at them. Did you see them rowing out like a couple of mad things to take it down?'

'No.'

She lowered her voice. 'I reckon one of the Volunteers put it up, but Mam is convinced it was one of the women in Cumann na mBan.'

'So, no one was got for it yet?' I asked.

'There were so many boats coming and going at the time, they haven't a clue.'

I felt someone's hand tapping my back. It was Terence.

'I've got to go.'

'You're going with Terence?' Maisie whispered.

'Have to,' I said.

A little stone bridge crossed the River Deel as it left the lake. Mr McSorley leaned against one of the walls, smoking his pipe.

'Ready for the job?' he asked.

'We are, Mr McSorley,' I said.

He paused, looking at us both intently over his glasses as he sucked his pipe. Then, holding it up in one hand, he pointed it at us.

'Lads, we're going on a job together. Drop the "mister".'

Terence was probably used to this but being asked to call Mr McSorley by his first name made me feel like I had been officially invited to join the world of grown-ups.

'Right, Malachy,' I said, feeling very grand indeed.

I watched our boat move closer to Nun's Island and my mind wandered back to the day when Dad had told me about the raid.

'They're after guns?' I said.

'That's right — in Norwood House and they need someone who's good at acting.' I could hear the proud tone in Dad's voice and asked him when was it planned for.

'That's a strange day to carry out a raid,' I said when I heard it was to happen on the day of the Sports.

'Not when you think of all the police who'll be busy at the lake. It's the perfect day for it,' he said.

And now the day had come. It was all very well to talk and

prepare, but this wasn't a practice. This wasn't a rehearsal for a play. This *was* the play, except it was real life and I was one of the real-life actors. I felt a lurch in my stomach.

Alice could barely be seen now. I imagined what it would be like if she walked along the lake road playing 'Brian Boru's March' on the whistle with the four us marching behind her towards Norwood House.

A cloud of dust moved down to the lake, as a car came towards us. It pulled up and Tom waved at us from behind the steering wheel. The three of us bundled in.

The road by the lake wove round many a bend and up many a hill. With all the twists and turns, Terence and I slid from side to side on the back seat. The smell of the leather inside and the motion of the car didn't agree with me. Waves of sickness in my stomach started in a small way, but came stronger and faster the further we travelled. I tried to think of a soothing song but couldn't stay with any tune. Maybe words would work better than music to settle it. I remembered the Master in school had once said the lake was like a mirror. I took those words now and kept saying 'lake like a mirror' as the road wound up into the hills, and we left 'the mirror' behind us. We hadn't gone far when Alice's voice made its way into my head saying:

'Mirror, mirror on the wall, who's the bravest of us all?'

'Not far to go now,' said Tom. Trees on both sides of the

road stretched over to meet in the middle as if we were driving through a leafy tunnel.

'Here we are,' said Tom. A stone cottage in a small clearing came into view on our right. He turned the car into the yard.

'Wait for me here, lads. I have to pay a visit to my tailor,' said Malachy.

'Could I get out for a minute?' I asked Tom.

'Are you all right?'

'Feeling a bit sick from the car.' I stepped outside and breathed in the fresh air, trying my best not to vomit. A black cat crept out from under an old cart in the corner of the yard. He slunk towards me and rubbed against my legs, then crossed in front of the car and into the house.

'There's our good luck for today,' said Tom.

Malachy emerged from the cottage ten minutes later, wearing a khaki jacket, trousers and cap, the uniform of the British Army. He walked like a soldier back towards us.

'Very fine tailor you have there, sir,' said Tom in an English accent.

'First-rate,' said Malachy, also in an English accent. Like Tom, he had worked in London before the war. Both had learned to drive there.

'Let's go through the plan,' said Tom. 'So, Terence and I are going to head up to the grove of trees beside the big house.'

'That's right,' said Terence. 'There's a shortcut to it from here.'

'In the meantime, Malachy and Colm will drive up and stop in front of the hall door. Malachy will drag Colm up the steps because he's knocked him off his bike. Once he and Colm get an entrance, we'll be in the door after them,' said Tom.

'And we go straight downstairs for the guns,' said Terence.

'I believe there are only two people in the house at the moment,' said Malachy.

'That's right: Miss Fernsby and her maid, Ivy McGill, so there shouldn't be any problem,' said Tom. 'She's a young slip of a girl from the Protestant Orphan Society.'

'She hardly gave information about where the guns are kept?' asked Malachy.

'No, that came from a girl in Cumann na mBan who used to help around the house a couple of times a week. She left for Liverpool yesterday so they'll not be bringing her in for questioning.'

'Once we get the rifles and put them in the car,' said Terence, 'Malachy and I take off through the woods in two different directions.'

'And Colm and I will drive off with the guns,' said Tom.

'Are we ready?' asked Malachy. Tom and Terence took masks made out of black stockings and tied them on.

'Let's go. Give us five minutes to get up there, Malachy!' said

Tom. Malachy checked his watch, then turned to me.

'Are you feeling all right? You look very pale,' he said.

I couldn't admit how bad I felt. He might think I was scared. He pulled the peak of his cap down further on his forehead and did the same with mine. It was time for the show to begin.

Chapter Sixteen

'Right, let's go,' said Malachy as he drove through the gate up the avenue past purple and pink rhododendrons. After turning a bend, the car bumped over a little humpback bridge — not helpful to the way I was feeling — and the big house came into view: a grey granite building, three storeys over a basement. About a dozen steps led up to the white front door. On each side were flowers and shrubs, all sorts of colours.

Malachy pulled up close to the steps. He hopped out and helped me out of the back seat.

'Act as if you're in a bad way,' he said. 'They could be watching us from a window.' There was very little acting in it for me. Malachy dragged me up to the front door and rang the bell.

The 'slip of a girl' peeked out through the barely opened door. If I had been told she was twelve years old, I'd have believed it.

'Sorry to disturb you, Miss,' said Malachy in an English accent. 'I was driving to the barracks in Oldcastle and this young lad came out of nowhere on his bike. Couldn't stop in time. Ran into him. You can see he's in a bad way, poor chap. Could you help us, please?'

A voice came from inside. 'Ivy?'

'There's a young boy after being hit by an army man in his car, Miss,' said Ivy.

I was counting the stone steps, hoping it would calm my stomach, but it was no use. I grabbed the railings and vomited into the flowerbed beyond them. What flowers I destroyed, I have no idea. But as I held onto the railings, I was relieved to find that my stomach started feeling better. I had a sense of a black dress coming out onto the top step. Malachy rubbed my back and swung around.

'My dear lady,' said Malachy, 'as you can see, we're in urgent need of assistance.'

'Quick, get him inside,' said Miss Fernsby. She stepped back into the hall first. Malachy put his arm around my shoulder and we plodded forwards. Within seconds, Tom had pushed past us, followed by Terence. They rushed through the hall and clomped down the stairs to the basement.

Miss Fernsby, her mouth open, watched the men go past. She checked Malachy's uniform again, trying to make sense of what she had seen.

'I beg your pardon?' she said to Malachy, who was now holding a gun.

'No need to beg, Madam,' said Malachy in his English accent. 'Would you mind stepping into the parlour, please?'

'How dare you take advantage of my good nature?' she

said sharply as she opened the parlour door. Two red blotches flared up on her cheeks.

'I'd advise you to remain quiet, Madam … You, Miss,' he said to Ivy. 'Follow your mistress. My friends and I will be leaving in a few minutes. We won't be staying for tea.' Ivy started to cry.

'Oh, for heaven's sake, girl,' said Miss Fernsby.

Once both women were inside, Malachy produced a key given to him by the woman who had left for Liverpool. He locked the door.

'Are you all right?' he asked me. I nodded. 'Good. I want you to get the handgun upstairs. We were told it's in a study. Go up the stairs, turn right and go to the last room on the right. You'll find it in the drawer of the desk.'

The parlour door started rattling.

'Where are you going?' screamed Miss Fernsby. 'You have no right to go up there.' She banged on the door with her fist. 'No right, no right!' Malachy nodded at me to keep going.

I climbed the stairs. The dark red carpet muffled my footsteps in the long corridor. All these rooms and only two people living in the house! Damp patches stained the wallpaper between the doors on my right. At the last door, I put my hand on the brass doorknob. A key in the keyhole on the inside rattled. I opened the door into a small study that smelled of musty books and furniture wax.

The shutters were closed, but not completely. A sliver of sunlight shone on the mahogany desk below the window. I pulled the metal handle of the drawer. Swollen with damp, it didn't budge. It took three rough tugs before it opened. A handgun nestled among some papers. I lifted it, my hand shaking. I could hear my own breathing as I tip-toed towards the door. A shuffling behind me stopped me taking a step further. Something else was in the room. It could be a rat, I told myself.

I chanced turning around. The light in the room was faint, but there was enough to see a man in a British Army uniform lying on the floor. His jacket was pulled tightly around his curled-up back and his whole body was shaking. I remembered a boy at a feis once who lay down on the floor of the hall and had a 'fit'. Could that be happening here?

There was no time to stand and wonder what was wrong with him. I had to get out while he was facing the other way. Keeping the gun out of sight, I continued towards the door. Suddenly it banged closed. I froze in fright. And if that wasn't bad enough, I felt a pair of hands grab hard at my leg.

'Are you French or German?' a voice whispered. I looked down. The man squinted his eyes and was searching my face as if trying to make out what or who I was. I pulled my leg but there was no letting go. I thought that it might be dangerous to admit to being Irish, so I said, 'I'm not German, sir.'

The soldier stared into my eyes, without blinking. He stopped shaking.

'*Parlez-vous Français?*' he asked.

'English?' I said to him.

'You're English? You must be one of the new recruits. I don't remember seeing you before. Have you come with a message from Captain Farrell?'

'Captain Farrell?' I repeated.

'For God's sake, boy, aren't you with the Leinsters? Didn't you come through the field of barbed wire?'

Did he think he was back in the war? Was that why he asked me was I French or German? I tried to pull away again, but his grip was too tight.

'Where are you going with that gun, boy?'

I was hoping he hadn't seen it. My only chance now was to go along with him.

'I was given orders to get it, sir,' I said.

'Orders from whom?'

I was about to make up a name when he started shaking again.

'Are you right?' came a shout from downstairs. Malachy was deliberately not using my name.

'Orders from the sergeant. That's him calling now,' I said.

'I don't like it, boy,' the soldier said. Then his voice dropped so low, I could hardly hear it. 'I think I heard the Germans running past, on their way to Hill 63.'

'You did, sir. That's why the sergeant needs this gun,' I said.

'What about Aunt Felicity?' he asked, my leg still in his tight grip.

'She's down there with the sergeant.'

'You mean the Germans could get her? O God! Aunt Felicity in the hands of the Hun! Boy, get down there at once.'

'Yes, sir,' I said. He let go of my leg and I dashed from the study, plucking the key from the keyhole as I passed. I closed the door and although my hands were shaking, I managed to lock it. I sped down the corridor and the stairs. Malachy was carrying four shotguns towards the door.

'What the hell kept you?' he asked. The soldier upstairs started banging at the door and shouting. Malachy stopped. 'Someone's upstairs?'

'A soldier. I've locked him into the study,' I said.

Malachy didn't get a chance to ask any other questions. Tom and Terence were on their way up from the basement, each of them carrying a couple of rifles.

'Did you get the rifle hidden in the leg of the trousers?' asked Malachy.

'We did, we did,' said Terence. They hurried out the door and I followed them. Miss Fernsby was still shouting.

'You'll be caught, you crowd of low—' The front door closed behind me.

126

As soon as we had all the guns in the back of the car, Tom threw an old coat over them. Not a word was spoken. Malachy and Terence took off into the woods. Tom pulled off his mask and started up the car. As we drove by the house, Miss Fernsby stood at the parlour window, shaking her fist. Her mouth was still moving, shouting threats at us. Upstairs, one shutter remained closed over the window of the study. On the side that was open, the soldier stood close to the windowpane, his face white and still like the statue of St Michael in the church. What was he thinking as he saw us drive away?

Chapter Seventeen

Travelling home was no different from the journey to Norwood House. My stomach churned without a minute's rest. And this time we had to drive a longer distance, as the arms dump was beyond Oldcastle. Tom stopped a couple of times, but as soon as I climbed back in, my stomach started retching again.

Back in Glenidan, Nan watched me stumble into the kitchen. One look at my pale face made her whip out one of her 'cures'. It was a bottle of murky green liquid that reminded me of the slimy pond in the Fort Field, and it smelled even worse. I suffered two spoonfuls and lay on Dad's bed, easing my way into the hollow section in the middle. Nan went out to do the milking and before the clock struck the hour, my stomach had settled. Maybe there was something to that vile liquid after all.

Come Wednesday evening, the adventure of the raid was fading into the background. The audition in Kells was now taking centre stage. Up in the parlour, I took my fiddle out. I closed the case and propped it up on the good chair, pretending it was an American sitting in front of me.

'You would like me to play a hornpipe? I'd be delighted,' I said. I put the fiddle up on my shoulder and placed the bow over the strings. I had played only half the tune when the door opened and Dad's face peered around it.

'What's this I hear about you taking on a soldier in Norwood House?' he asked.

I put my fiddle back into the case.

'We were told there were only two people in the house, the two women,' I said. 'Malachy told me to go upstairs to get a handgun from a desk. I did that, but as I was leaving the room, a man stepped out from behind the door and asked me what I was doing.' I made sure to stick to the version I had given Tom and Malachy. 'He was a soldier.'

'What did you do?' Dad asked.

'I reminded him that I was the person with the gun and he'd better be careful,' I said.

'Never! What happened next?'

'I told him to stand aside and let me through. He didn't want to do it, but he had no choice. There was a key in the door. Before he knew what was going on, I was the far side of the door, locking it.'

'And did he not do anything to stop you?' asked Dad.

'Not one thing. He seemed to be very nervous once he saw

I had a gun,' I said.

'Well, everybody's talking about it. Tom was telling me that the man was roaring to be let out when ye were all leaving.'

'He was screaming and banging the door,' I said. That much was true anyway.

'That was some feat, lad,' he said, giving me a big pat on the back. 'Joe Kennedy heard about it and he insists on bringing you to your appointment on Saturday.'

'In a car?' I asked.

'Of course,' said Dad.

I knew that my version of what had happened in Norwood House was mostly made up. But at that moment, it was worth every lying word that came out of my mouth; not for the lift in the car to Kells, but for that pat on the back from Dad.

'Now, tell me about Sports Day,' said Dad. 'How did everything go?'

Come Saturday morning, a Ford car drove out of the yard. Tom was behind the wheel and Joe Kennedy sat beside him. I sat in the back, my fiddle in its black shiny case beside me. To avoid the sickness that had plagued me the last time, I had a word with Tom to drive slowly. Joe was all right with this too, but he wasn't the best of timekeepers, and as we drove down the boreen out onto the road, we were a half an hour behind time.

'I'm meeting some of the Sinn Féin club at the Town Hall,' Joe said to me. 'We'll park the motor car there and you can go down to the Saint Vincent De Paul Hall.' He turned back to Tom.

'Did I tell you about the dance in the Temperance Hall in Kilskyre?'

'Was that after the bazaar?' asked Tom.

The talk about Kilskyre took off. In the back of the car, my mind had wandered to the tunes in my head. The fingers on my left hand were twitching as I played the 'Green Fields', not along a country road in the Irish midlands, but in a fancy theatre in New York, with electric lights and hundreds of soft seats with Americans sitting on them, and long red velvet curtains each side of a big stage. Their clapping at the end of my hornpipe would mean I'd have to take several bows. And to top it all, I was going to be paid for it.

'Colm!' a voice interrupted my daydream. I had to leave the luxurious picture house in New York and come back to the car as it crawled up the hill of Crossakiel.

'We were talking about your grandfather the other day,' said Joe. 'He was a great man for the IRB. Had to skip it to America at one stage too. I'm sure you know all about that. Worked for the cause over there, my own father told me. Then he came back to take over the farm in Glenidan.'

'Did he?' I answered. I had been told that he was in the IRB, but nothing about going to America. I realised that I knew very little about my mother's father.

'If you get this job, we might enlist *you* for the cause in America,' said Joe, turning around to me.

'There's no "might" in it. I'd definitely sign up,' I answered.

'Good lad,' said Joe.

Working for the cause in America could be even more exciting than joining the Volunteers. If my own grandfather did it, maybe it was laid out for me to do the same.

We passed by the spire of Loyd, the lighthouse above in the hills, miles away from the sea. The two men up front started talking about the Kells races; normally they were held up there, but there were none this year so far. Something to do with Sinn Féin prisoners, according to Joe, but at that moment, all I cared about was that Kells was very close now. Tom started slowing down.

'What's this?' asked Joe.

Two policemen stood on the road, waving their arms. One pointed to where he wanted Tom to park the car. He motioned to us to get out. We stood in a row on the side of the road.

'Are you Michael Joseph Kennedy of Castlepollard, Co. Westmeath?' asked one of the policemen.

'I am,' said Joe.

'Then I'm arresting you for seditious words spoken by

you at a meeting in—'

'Seditious words at a meeting? On what grounds were any of my words seditious? I demand to—'

'With all due respect, Mr Kennedy,' said the policeman. 'You may express your *demands* to the magistrate. We are not authorised to listen to or act upon the likes of your *demands* on the public road.'

There was a chariot parked beside the ditch, facing the town. The policeman ordered us to get into it.

'There's no need to detain the driver or this young man. Please let them go,' said Joe.

'We are under instructions to bring you, and anyone with you, in for questioning,' said the policeman. 'Just following orders, Mr Kennedy. Just following orders.'

Chapter Eighteen

'So, this is British justice is it?' complained Joe. 'Bringing innocent men and young boys in and subjecting them to questioning without any evidence?'

'Like I said, Mr Kennedy, keep your speeches for the magistrate,' said the policeman leading us over to his truck.

We sat in silence as the chariot drove up Climber Hall and turned right into the barracks yard. As we walked towards the door of the barracks, Joe decided to try his luck with the other policeman.

'Constable, this young man has a very important appointment at eleven o'clock. He is—'

'You've got an even more important appointment in fifteen minutes, Mr Kennedy,' he answered. 'We will deal with this young man in our own time, thank you.'

Joe gave me a sympathetic look. I thought about breaking away and running down the hill, but only a fool would take such a chance. There were policemen everywhere and I wouldn't get farther than the gate. I followed the others into the barracks. The room we were ushered into had a strong smell of beer and we could hear a man singing 'A Nation Once Again' as he was being escorted to a cell. I sat on the bench, my fiddle beside me. So much for my big chance! I stood up, sat down, walked to the opposite wall and sat down on the bench there. I decided to go up to the hatch myself and ask if I could go.

The two policemen who had brought us in were talking to each other. I stood and waited. Neither of them turned around. I cleared my throat. Still no reaction.

'Excuse me, Constables,' I said finally. 'I have an appointment in the Saint Vincent de Paul Hall to play my fiddle for an American filmmaker. It was supposed to be at eleven o'clock.'

The two men turned to the clock. It was almost twenty-five past eleven.

'One minute,' said the older one. He walked out and spoke to another person in a room nearby. The younger man sat down at the desk and started sorting through a pile of papers.

The other policeman came back in.

'You may go, young man,' he said.

I flew out the door past Joe and Tom, hardly giving them a chance to wish me good luck.

Cannon Street was quiet, but come Newmarket Street, I had to weave in and out through droves of shoppers. It was market day, after all. Nulty's on the far side looked busy. Passing the windows full of scrapbooks, men's watches, books of music and maps was a first for me! Two men came out of McEntee's Bar and Grocery further down. I thought I heard one of them speaking Irish as he made his way into the butcher's next door, but I kept going. Down the hill to Back Street, moving as fast as I could holding a violin case, I tried to avoid bumping into people on the street. The gate into the hall was still open. In the little courtyard, a man in a black suit was leaning against the door of the billiards room.

'You're coming to see the Yank about the music?' he asked.

'Yes.'

'Sorry, lad,' he said. 'He left about ten minutes ago.' He was about to go back inside when he stopped. 'He's staying in the Headfort Arms. Why don't you go over and see if he's still there?'

The Headfort Arms Hotel was only across the road. I might still be in with a chance. I dashed across and inside. A fair-haired woman at the desk was writing in a ledger. She half-glanced at me.

'Excuse me,' I said.

She stopped and forced a 'Yes?'

'Is the man from J.D. Pictures still in the hotel?'

She dipped her pen into the inkwell and started writing again. A maid in a black dress came up behind me with a silver teapot, a cup and saucer and a jug on a silver tray. She smiled at me as she placed it on the desk. The woman ignored her.

'Gone,' she said, her head still down over her work.

'Have you any idea where he's gone to?' I asked.

The woman put down her pen.

'We don't discuss the whereabouts of our guests,' she said and she looked down at my jacket as if it was going to infect her.

I turned around and walked out through the entrance, but as I did, someone tapped me on the arm. It was the maid who had delivered the tray. She closed the door behind her.

'This morning at breakfast I heard him say he was taking the quarter to twelve train to Oldcastle when he was finished,' she whispered and disappeared back into the hotel again before I could thank her.

I dashed to a spot outside the nearby Medical Hall. Through the trees across the road, I was able to see the clock over the Girls' National School. All the flying around like a bluebottle in the past twenty minutes was in vain. The clock read a quarter to twelve exactly. I could imagine the man from J.D. Pictures climbing onto the Oldcastle train, cursing the boy who hadn't shown up in the hall. How I wished I could stretch over and put the hands of that clock back by an hour. Then I could cross the road and play my tunes in the hall instead of wandering back to the entrance of the Headfort Arms Hotel in a quandary as to what to do next. All those foolish dreams of playing in New York and I couldn't even get to a hall in Ireland on time!

A couple crossed the road from the chapel and turned to go

into the hotel. I had to move aside to let them through. The woman, in a flowery dress, was laughing at some joke the man had told her. He walked past and grinned at me as if I should be part of whatever funny story he was telling. I turned away. How could anyone laugh today?

What could I do now? Pick up my violin case and walk back up to the barracks? There was no other choice. I tried to get a tune going in my head as I made my way up Back Street. That usually helped but, as if someone had cast a spell of silence over that fiddle, no music came.

Chapter Nineteen

By the time the Volunteers were setting up the stage for Mrs Sheehy Skeffington in the Square in Castle-pollard, three weeks later, my 'Kells fiasco', as Joe Kennedy referred to it, was beginning to fade into the past. Joe kept telling me how bad he felt, and he promised to scour the newspaper ads every week. Tom was the same and he even wrote to a cousin in America, asking was there anything doing. As for me, missing the chance to play in Kells was like sliding down the longest snake in a game of 'Snakes and Ladders'; and looking ahead, no ladders were in sight.

Even Dad felt sorry for me.

'The reception and the aeraíocht are coming up soon. That'll cheer you up,' he said.

So here I was in Castlepollard, close to six o'clock. Dad had said he'd meet me at five at the railings of the Protestant Church. For the umpteenth time, I scanned the crowd, but still no sign of him. More and more bodies poured into the square for the reception. A local group of Sinn Féiners, holding a banner with the words 'Sinn Féin Abú' written on it, pushed through the hordes of people. Some of the men had the Sinn Féin badges we sold before the election pinned to the lapels of their jackets. Close on their heels were the Volunteers, half of them in smart green uniforms, the other half dressed as close to the uniform as possible. Every man wore a Volunteer cap, and beneath each peak, a serious face gazed steadily ahead. Tom Cooke headed up the Glenidan Corps, a tricolour flag held over his shoulder. I couldn't help but think of my dream, when I saw him.

The Cumann na mBan followed in their belted khaki jackets and their green felt hats. Lizzie Scarlett — the nurse who had warned us that day outside the church in Collinstown — and her sister Katie held a tricolour banner with the words 'Cumann na mBan' embroidered onto it. They all marched out the Mullingar road to welcome the visitors who were arriving in a pony and brake.

About a dozen policemen stood outside McQuestions' house at the corner, never speaking to each other, and constantly watching what was going on around them. Two others stood close by at the church gate.

'Hey Colm!' I heard a voice shout. It was Peter. He and Patsy were walking with their mother towards the Mullingar Road. 'I'll catch up with you,' he told them and came over to me.

'Well, did you bring it?'

I patted the pocket of my jacket.

'I did, indeed.'

Little did the policemen standing a few feet away from us know that a whistle belonging to the force was in my pocket.

'We need to keep a close eye on the Reillys tomorrow,' said Peter.

'Yes, and make sure we're on the road home before them.'

'That whistle will scare the living daylights out of them,' said Peter, chuckling. 'I can't wait to see their faces.'

'Are they here today?'

'Are you joking? Their mother wouldn't let them come to something like this. Are you coming out the Mullingar Road?'

'No, I've to meet Dad here.'

'Come on, Peter!' called his mother over to him.

'Are you staying for the speeches?' I asked.

'Can't,' said Peter, moving away. 'Mam thinks it's too dangerous.' He gave me a friendly punch on the shoulder and off he went with his mother and brother. I watched him go and wondered what that was like — to go down a road, walking with your mother in the middle and your younger brother the far side. But I was jolted back to the present when I heard a familiar voice.

'Excuse me, please.' Mrs Dobbs from the post office was pushing through the crowd. A smell of brown bread wafted from her basket.

'Look at them,' she said to one of the policemen. 'Erecting a stage in a public street for the likes of those rabble-rousers.'

'Are you not a Shinner then?' he asked, smiling.

'Good Lord, no! Home Rule is good enough for the likes of me, who lives in the *real* world. I'm proud to say I've been an Irish Party woman all my life. God be good to John Redmond. *There* was a real politician — not like yon crowd of Rainbow Chasers.'

'So, what has you here today?'

Mrs Dobbs patted her basket.

'I'm trying to get over to Chapel Street to deliver a cake of brown bread to an old friend. The poor woman is terrified to leave her own home with all the hooligans in town.'

'Don't delay on the way,' said the policeman. 'We're expecting trouble.'

'I can assure you, I'll not be delaying, and I won't be in a hurry back either.'

Still no sign of Dad. The church bell rang, and there were mutterings of people saying the Angelus. It wasn't like Dad to be this late and not send word.

A faint sound of the Oldcastle Brass Band playing in the distance could be heard from the direction of the Mullingar Road. Our special visitors must be arriving. The drumbeat got louder and the tune 'God Save Ireland' filled the air. Both sides of the road were lined with people cheering and clapping. The band was getting louder; I could almost feel the pulse of the big bass drum beat in my own body, even though I couldn't see it with the crowd swelling all the time.

It was at that point I spotted Terence McKay, pushing through the crowd towards the railings. He was in Volunteer uniform, seeking me out to lord it over me, no doubt. Dad had warned me not to go into the Square, but it looked like he wasn't coming. I could see Terence hadn't seen me yet, so I made up my own mind about what to do. Before he took another step, I decided, by gum, it was my time to leave.

Chapter Twenty

I took off and tunnelled through the crowd in the Square, in the direction of the platform that had been specially built onto the front wall of the Pollard Arms. I was well capable of scarpering if there was any trouble. What I didn't bargain for was how close people stood to each other. The further I burrowed, the harder I had to press past the bulky legs and skirts, as space was getting scarcer all the time. I knew by the heat, the closeness of the men, and the smell of sweat that I was coming close to the platform.

The music was very loud now. People were clapping and cheering and making way for the band members to march through. A pony and brake came next with five people in it. Two women wearing glasses sat beside each other. They both wore black straw hats. A younger woman sat beside them wearing a green hat. Joe Kennedy sat opposite and to one side of him was a man I didn't recognise. This must be Jack O'Sheehan.

The Volunteers marched behind them. Tom Cooke came forward with the tricolour and stood to attention as Joe and the visitors climbed down from the brake and up the steps to the platform. I was about three rows back until two women from the Gaelic League noticed me and pushed me out front to give me a better view — and pushed me accidentally straight into Tom Cooke, nearly making him drop the flag.

'What in the name of God are you doing here?'

'I've the same right as anyone to see what's going on,' I said to him.

'Not when you've been warned there could be trouble,' he said, his mouth so close to my ear that I could feel his breath.

'Dad never showed up,' I said.

'I'm sure there was a good reason for that.'

He herded me through the Volunteers who stood stoutly in front of the platform and pushed me underneath.

'Stay there until the speeches are over,' he said.

The top of my head brushed off the platform overhead. At least it was cooler in here. The smell of fresh wood and sawdust reminded me of the workshop at home. I sank onto the soft ground and stared out at the men; I was only able to see as far as their chests.

One of the Volunteers called 'hush' to the men beside him and that hush spread over the crowd. The stage above me vibrated with footsteps and, within seconds, you could hear a sixpence drop in the grass, as the crowd waited for someone to talk. Sure enough, Joe Kennedy's booming voice filled the square. He was welcoming an American journalist who was here to witness what was *really* going on. She was tired of reading accounts in the newspapers that were censored by the British. He finished his speech by saying: 'And before Mrs Sheehy Skeffington addresses us, it's my great pleasure to welcome our first speaker, recently released from prison, Mr Jack O'Sheehan.'

The clapping, shouting and hooting that greeted these words echoed for miles.

Jack O'Sheehan must have raised his hand or shown in some way that he was about to talk, as the crowd went quiet.

'Fellow Rainbow Chasers…' This was greeted by some laughs in the crowd. 'As many of you know, I was given two years' hard labour for singing "The Felons in our Land" and "The Soldiers' Song".'

I could hear a man's voice shouting up from where the policemen were standing:

'Stop right there! I am District Inspector Foley. This meeting has been proclaimed by the Crown and must hereby come to an end.'

This was met by hisses from the crowd. These quickly turned into loud groans and finally into even louder 'boos'. I moved further under the platform, closer to the wall of the hotel. The boos faded out and the crowd went quiet again.

'If you're talking about this,' said Joe Kennedy. 'It states clearly that the Aeraíocht has been banned.' He must have held up one of the notices that were posted up all around the town the night before, announcing that the aeraíocht was not allowed to go ahead. 'It doesn't say anything about this evening's reception.'

'You tell him, Joe,' shouted a voice from the crowd.

'As far as the law is concerned, *this* is part of that illegal gathering,' said the Inspector. 'If you continue your speeches, I'm going to have to take action because you are breaking the law.'

'Breaking whose law?' said a woman's voice above me. This must have been Mrs Sheehy Skeffington.

'Not our law,' shouted a voice further away.

With that, the crowd started cheering and clapping. I could hear the Inspector shouting, 'Order them to disperse!'

Somebody was coming down the steps. At ground level, I saw that it was Joe. He was holding Mrs Sheehy Skeffington's elbow as he led her into the hotel. Jack O'Sheehan followed, helping his wife and the woman in the green hat, who must have been the American. Six or seven policemen pushed through the Volunteers, ran up the steps onto the platform and shouted, 'Disperse, disperse!'

The Volunteers stood their ground, but the men and women behind them started running in all directions, like cattle going wild on a fair day. This was because several more policemen came from God knows where and rushed towards the Volunteers, belting them with their batons. When I looked again, I realised that it wasn't only the RIC; soldiers had arrived as well. Men were putting up their hands to protect their heads from the battering. *Thwack!* Tom was on the ground near the steps of the platform, one side of his head bleeding. Another Volunteer pulled him up and helped him away.

I could hear the rattle of the boots of the policemen above me.

'Get them, lads!' shouted a man's voice from the crowd. This was followed by the clatter of stones on the wooden stage, like hailstones on the galvanised roof of the dairy at home, except a hundred times louder.

'This is how the British treat small nations,' shouted a woman close to the platform. It was a deep voice. I'd swear it was Lizzie Scarlett's. Another shower of stones was hurled at the policemen from the crowd, banging on the wood over-head. I lay on the ground and covered my ears. How was I ever going to get out?

I turned around to discover that I wasn't on my own any-more. A soldier was crawling in the sawdust. He stopped face down, putting his hands over the back of his head. I thought he might be injured first, but there was something familiar about the way his jacket stretched on his back. He took his hands off his head and slid around to face me, brushing off some saw-dust from his chin and nose. But it was the glazed look in the eyes that brought me back to the window in Norwood House where I had last seen them staring at me.

'Did you hear the German guns?' he shouted.

'I think it's only stones being thrown onto the stage,' I said.

'Wait a minute; I know you,' he said, raising himself up. He knelt in front of me, eyes searching my face. His hand shook as it moved towards me and gripped my arm. There was no point shouting for help with the din that was going on around us. I tried to pull away, but there was no letting go, no more than that Sunday evening in Norwood House.

'I remember you from the trenches at Ypres,' he said. 'You were bringing a message from Captain Farrell. O God! Don't tell me!'

'It couldn't have been me,' I said. 'I wasn't there.'

'Don't lie to me,' he said, shaking my arm roughly. 'I remember you! I know why you're here.' I tried to move away again; his fingers were digging into my skin. I wanted to scream. What on earth could I say? He came up close to my ear.

'It's the order to go over the top, isn't it?'

He started shaking, but still held onto me.

'We're going to hear the signal any minute?' he said. 'Listen!'

A man shouted in Irish. 'Time to stop. Time to give up before somebody gets badly hurt.'

'That must be one of the Germans,' he said to me. 'They're so close.'

'That isn't German, it's Irish,' I said, hoping that would calm him.

'Irish? You're out of your mind. You think you're back in Dublin when that crowd of troublemakers took over the G.P.O. Wake up, boy! We're in Ypres and the Germans are yards away! Brace yourself! We're going to be told to climb out any minute and face them.'

He held my arm so tightly that I felt it was about to break.

'The signal — they're going to give the signal…' he closed his eyes and dropped his head onto his chest.

How was I to handle this? Signal, signal … I don't know why, but it came into my mind that I once heard someone say that a whistle was blown to tell the soldiers to get out of the trenches and into battle with the Germans. That gave me an idea.

'Nobody's going to give the signal,' I said, taking the whistle out of my pocket.

'What's that?'

'It's the whistle — it's the signal. Once *you* have the whistle, nobody else can blow it.'

He snatched it from me and let go of my arm. Before I had a chance to move away, he grabbed my hand.

'Thank you, soldier,' he said, shaking it and squeezing my fingers tightly for a few seconds. He dropped my hand and examined the whistle.

I moved away from him. My legs were unsteady, but I wanted to have a look out to see what was happening. More and more soldiers were filling the square. Facing the crowd, they formed a line across in front of the platform.

'Ready, take aim...' shouted one of the soldiers above me. I held onto one of the posts of the platform. Dad could be out there — so could many others I knew. Were the soldiers going to stand and fire out on a crowd? Something like this happened years ago; the Castlepollard Massacre people called it. People were fired on at a fair day. Was that going to happen now? But a change came over the crowd. In those few seconds, it seemed like every person in the Square drew in their breath. The sight of those guns stopped all the shouting, shoving and stone-throwing.

'Hold your fire!' shouted the same voice. The soldiers stood as if turned to stone. Now I could see a clear passage towards the main door of the hotel. I took my chance and made a run for it. The barman was about to close the door over, as he always did when there was any trouble around.

'Colm!' He bundled me in, slammed the doors closed and put the bar across. 'Into the snug. Quick!'

I opened the door of the snug and dropped onto the long bench. I closed my eyes but only for seconds; the sound of the door opening sharply gave me a jolt. Terence McKay walked in and stood in front of me.

'Well, if it isn't the hero of the Norwood House raid,' he said.

'Sh... What do you want?' I asked.

'That looked like an interesting conversation you were having with that soldier outside,' he said in a low voice.

'Interesting? I'd hardly call it that,' I said.

'What would you call it, then?' asked Terence.

'I'd call it "none of your business",' I replied.

'Your business was to be at the railings of the bank to meet your father. Where on earth were you? I went looking for you at six o'clock.'

'I was there. Waited for ages. Didn't think he was coming,' I said. 'What did you want?'

'Only to tell you that he couldn't make it. He said to meet him back in Tom Cooke's.' Terence backed out and closed the door. I lay down on the bench and closed my eyes. I'd go to Tom's as soon as it was safe to leave the Pollard Arms and not a second sooner.

Chapter Twenty-One

Up to now, all the talk was about the reception, about the stones and the guns and the fright everybody had. Malachy was relieved that the members of the band from Oldcastle had been able to get into the hotel before things turned ugly.

'We have to put it behind us now and get our plans up and running for tomorrow,' said Joe.

Tom Cooke pushed through the crowd of people in his kitchen. Lizzie Scarlett, putting her nursing skills to good use, had wound a bandage around his head.

'Not too late for the potato cakes?' he asked.

'Five minutes, Tom,' said Nuala, turning around. 'You haven't lost your appetite, so that's a good sign.' The dripping on the big black pan sizzled as she shaped the last of the potato cakes on the floury kitchen table. The first batch hit the pan and smelled so delicious, I was tempted to sneak over and steal one. Nobody made potato cakes like Nuala Cooke.

Joe Kennedy stood at the head of the table, a sheet of paper in his hand. He pointed at an empty chair and Tom sat down.

'Before I start,' said Joe to the American journalist, 'there was a telephone message at the hotel for you, Miss.' He handed her a note. She made a clicking sound as she read it.

'That's from my fiancé,' she said. 'He can't come to Castle-pollard tonight. Instead, he'll meet us at the aeraíocht tomorrow.'

Joe sat down and took a pencil out of the breast pocket of his jacket.

'We drew up a number of items at a brief meeting in the hotel. First, the new venue.'

The parlour door opened. Mrs Sheehy Skeffington peeped in.

'I believe that's my cue to enter stage left,' she said. She stood in the doorway, fingering a gold brooch on the collar of her blouse.

'Mrs Sheehy Skeffington will explain what I mean by "new venue",' said Joe.

'Last week, Jack O'Sheehan and I were to speak in Cush-endun up on the coast of County Antrim, but the meeting was proclaimed,' she began. 'The place was swarming with police and soldiers. We let it be known to all the military men that we'd talk at another location and made sure that it was a difficult one to get to. The truth is that we weren't the ones who went to the new location; it was a group of people pretending to be us. Sure enough, the police and military took the bait and followed those "actors" through the hills and bogs of the glens of Antrim. In the meantime, we managed to slip out of Cushendun, travel over the mountain and speak in the Diamond in Ballycastle to a large and, I might add, a very enthusiastic crowd.'

'You're telling us you convinced the police the meeting was happening in one place, when in fact it was happening somewhere else?' asked Tom.

'That's right,' said Mrs Sheehy Skeffington. 'And in the light of what happened to us today, a few of us who met in the hotel afterwards thought we should follow a similar course of action here. In the "drama" tomorrow, Molly O'Sheehan is going to play the part of … well … myself. She was up on the stage with me and the police couldn't be sure which of us is Hanna Sheehy Skeffington. Joe's cousin, Henry — who I believe owes him several favours — is coming from Edgeworthstown to play the part of Jack O'Sheehan.'

'He'd better be very good looking,' said Jack O'Sheehan.

'What about me?' asked the American journalist. 'Who is going to play Jacinta C. Malone?'

'We're putting it around that you had to leave early, Miss Malone,' said Joe Kennedy. 'So, we won't be holding auditions for your part. The drama will start in the morning when the actors will leave the hotel to attend second Mass in Castlepollard. After that, they'll be brought around the town and back to the hotel for a cup of tea.'

'Who's going to bring them around?' asked Tom.

'Luke Weldon,' said Joe. 'The RIC know he's a Sinn Féin supporter.'

'I've organised a group of women to follow them around,' said Nuala, standing up at the hearth. 'We *must* have a crowd going after them. That'll make it all the more convincing.'

'Good, Nuala. Start by having them ready at the church after Mass,' said Joe. 'You can be sure the plainclothes police will be among the faithful in the chapel. In the meantime, Mrs Sheehy Skeffington, Mr O'Sheehan and Miss Malone will all stay here tonight.'

'Boy, this is simply delightful,' said Miss Malone. 'Wait until I write about this for the folks back in the States. I can see the headline: "Police brought on Wild Goose Chase" and the sub-headline: "Irish Patriots take to the Hills".'

'Coming back to the new venue,' said Joe. 'We've secured Brady's field up in the hills between Lough Glore and the White Lake.'

'Bradys of Johnstown?' asked Tom.

'Yes,' said Malachy. 'The lads are going to nail a piece of white ribbon onto the bark of the sycamore tree at the top of the boreen so people will know.'

Joe crossed 'venue' off his agenda.

'What about a stage?' he asked, underlining the next word.

Tom had the answer for him: 'The two bars in Fore said they'd send over barrels in the morning. The Lynches are bringing planks. Ned said he'd put it all together.'

'Bars?' asked Miss Malone.

'As in "saloons",' said Tom.

The pencil scratched off 'stage'.

'Good,' said Joe. 'Now, musicians, singers, dancers?'

'We've got runners on their way to them all. Katie, in the priest's house, is going to telephone Mrs Joyce,' said Dad. 'She'll get in touch with the judges for the competitions. They're coming from Mullingar. A couple of the Volunteers will take care of them.'

Joe crossed that off.

'The public at large,' he read from his list.

'The Volunteers are on the road as we speak,' said Dad, 'letting all their members around Castlepollard know. Lizzie Scarlett and the women from Cumann na mBan are out in the barn, carving up the area around Fore and Collinstown. The women have their bikes ready and will be off as soon as they've got their plan in place.'

'And I'll be going to Oldcastle tonight,' said Malachy. 'I'll put the word out there.'

'Who will collect us to bring us to the new venue?' asked Jack O'Sheehan.

'Terence McKay and myself,' said Dad. Terence waved his hand from where he was standing.

'Will I give you a hand there?' he asked Nuala when he saw

her taking plates down from the dresser.

'Would you mind handing out the food?'

The smell of the potato cakes put a smile on everyone's face. Terence passed by a few minutes later and handed a plate of them, topped with a little pool of melted butter, to Miss Malone.

She turned to me as she balanced a mouthful on a fork. 'What about you, young man? What's your job tomorrow?'

'Music's my job,' I said. 'I'm playing the fiddle for a competition and for the Irish dancers.'

'A fiddle player! Jasper — that's the guy who couldn't join us this evening — has been on the hunt for fiddle players. He needs them for a movie he's making.'

'Is he anything to do with J.D. Pictures?' asked Malachy.

'That's him,' said Miss Malone. 'J.D. stands for Jasper Delaney.'

'I tried to get to Kells to play for him,' I told her.

'All my fault,' said Joe, his mouth full of potato cake. 'I had Colm in the car when I was stopped by the RIC on the way to Kells and that's why he didn't make it.'

'That's too bad,' said Miss Malone.

'Has he filled all the places?' I asked.

'He has,' said Miss Malone.

'It's a shame he didn't hear Colm,' said Malachy. 'That lad can draw nectar from the flowers with his fiddle playing. You can make up your own mind when you hear him tomorrow.'

'I will, you can bet on it,' said Miss Malone, smiling at me. I didn't feel like smiling. If I had made it to Kells and got the job, everything would be different. I'd be looking forward to meeting my new boss tomorrow instead of being reminded of the chance that had been snatched from me.

Chapter Twenty-Two

There was a rap on the window.

'The women are off,' Nuala announced.

'Right-ee-o,' said Joe. 'Colm, will you check with Tom outside if the coast is clear to go back into town?'

I scurried out the door, leaving the brightly lit kitchen full of chatter. Outside, Nuala's roses, climbing over the arch at the gate, filled the evening air with perfume. A corncrake was croaking in the meadow nearest to the house. The beech tree that had fallen during the storm a few weeks earlier had left a gap in the hedge. Only a stump remained and Tom sat on the stile beside it, stroking his moustache. He was watching the last of the women cycling towards Castlepollard.

'It was powerful to see the women taking off on their bikes,' he said as I crossed the road. 'I'm sorry my mother didn't live to see this day. She was a member of the Ladies' Land League in Fore, back in the time of the Land War.'

He walked with me back towards the house.

'Back in the time of Parnell?' I asked.

'That's right. I was only a child and the women took on to raise money for evicted families. I remember going to a bazaar in Fore.'

'Where was it held?' I asked.

'The grounds of the church — and it made a pretty penny for the Land League. Someone donated a silver watch for the raffle, and the tickets sold like wildfire. If she were alive today, she'd have been one of the first to sign up for Cumann na mBan.'

We walked along the gravel path through the garden.

'Of course, she was a cousin of your granny's. That's one thing we can say about our family: each generation does their bit. If your mother was alive, God rest her, she'd be in Cumann na mBan too.'

I was thinking of the photo of my mother sitting solemnly on her wedding day. What would she look like in a Cumann na mBan uniform? I pictured her coming into Tom and Nuala's kitchen, sitting at the table and chatting with Mrs Shechy Skeffington.

'What about Uncle Kit?'

'He'd be in the Volunteers if he had lived. Sure, isn't the "cause" in our blood?'

Back inside, we let Joe know that it was safe to leave. He rounded up Mrs O'Sheehan and a few of the men. Nuala curled her arms around Mrs Sheehy Skeffington and Miss Malone's waists and ushered them back to the parlour. Hunger drew me over to the fire. One sad leftover sat in the pan. I scooped it up onto a plate, sat down at the end of the table, and ate it with my fingers. It didn't have melted butter, but I didn't care.

Dad checked the kettle to see if it had enough water for tea. He hung it on the crane and took his place back at the table. I sat at the other end, propping up my head with my hands, trying to stay awake.

'I believe your father fought in the war,' said Jack O'Sheehan to Terence.

'That's right,' said Terence.

'What's he doing with himself these days?' asked Jack.

Terence got up and took some cups and saucers down from the dresser. Would he say anything about his father?

'This and that,' said Terence.

Jack O'Sheehan nodded and waited for Terence to continue. Terence paused, then put out the jug of milk and the sugar bowl. The door opened and the subject of Terence's father closed. Nuala shuffled into the kitchen, dragging a bulging flour sack.

'Sorry to interrupt the chat, but I've a few more blankets for the bedding in the loft.'

'I'll bring it,' I said, glad of the excuse to leave. I took the sack and worked my way slowly through the yard. When my eyes got used to the dark, I moved faster. Once inside the barn, I dumped the bag beside the ladder. The extra blankets were for Terence and, by gum, he could bring them up himself.

My hands groped for the rungs of the ladder and my feet worked out where to go. I crawled onto the loft, gathered up a bundle of hay and tossed it into one corner. I felt along the floor for the blanket I had had last night and wrapped it around myself.

Sleep came fast, but it was a restless sleep, a sleep where voices outside the barn could easily wake me up. I sat up with a start. There were men outside. After a minute, I realised that it was Terence talking.

'I felt I had to tell you what I saw.'

'Let me get the story right,' said the other voice. It was Dad's. 'He was under the stage and met a British soldier. He talked to him for a few minutes and then gave him something?'

'And the worst thing was, they shook hands when the deal was done.'

Dad gave a little laugh.

'Are you sure it was Colm? He's as loyal to the cause as any of us. I couldn't see him doing any shady deal with a British soldier.'

'It was Colm all right,' said Terence. 'Sure, didn't I follow him into the hotel myself? If it wasn't shady, why didn't he mention anything about it to you?'

Dad didn't answer.

'Well, he's your son,' continued Terence. 'I'm sure you know best. I felt it was important, as a Volunteer, to report what I saw.'

'Report? Have you told this to anyone else?'

'Of course, I haven't, Seán. I meant report to *you*.'

'Don't say a word about this to anyone, Terence.'

I wrapped the blanket closer around me as I heard them coming up the ladder. There was no point in saying anything now. Did Terence really believe that I was in cahoots with a British soldier? Or was he using what he saw to set Dad — and maybe the Volunteers — against me?

I thought about Terence's own father, Bernard McKay. He had answered 'the call to colours' when the recruiting men from the British Army were busy in Castlepollard at the start of the war. Rumours were flying about in the summer of 1916 that he was spotted among wounded soldiers in a hospital in London. Did he ever go back to the war? Nobody knew. He was never reported killed or missing in action, but he never came home. People stopped asking Terence or his mother about him. Why would they want to add to their pain? Of course, Jack O'Sheehan, not being local, didn't know any better when he was asking about Terence's father this evening, especially in front of the rest of us.

If Terence had left me alone after he'd finished school, I'd have let bygones be bygones. I'd even have felt sorry for him. But the grudge he held against me was no ordinary grudge. It was like one of those growths that made Nan shake her head and bite her lip. She knew it was there to stay and none of her cures would make a blind bit of difference to it. In the past, it had been a mystery as to why Terence came after me. Peter put it down to jealousy; his Irish would never match mine. But there was more to it than that. I was beginning to think it was for having a father around while his never returned. *He's never going to change*, I told myself. As my eyelids began to droop, my mind was set on talking to Dad the first chance that came my way. He had heard Terence's side of the story; now it was time for him to hear mine.

Chapter Twenty-Three

I n spite of all I had heard, sleep did come — a sleep so deep that I was unaware when Dad and Terence left early in the morning. I even wondered had I dreamed about overhearing their chat the night before. But at Mass in Fore Chapel, snatches of what was said came back as clear as the stream that flowed through the valley. I hadn't dreamed it. Terence was not going to get away with this. I would have to talk to Dad today.

After Mass, Tom and Nuala's pony and trap trotted along the road, one of many. It was a typical line of traffic, but each pony was surprised when the driver drove past its usual turn-off. One by one, we passed the white-ribboned sycamore tree and made our way up the boreen into the hills. A man in a long tan overcoat and tweed cap was walking his bicycle uphill along that little road.

'Who's that?' asked Nuala.

Tom glanced over.

'Don't know him, but I wouldn't worry. There'll be men above at the gate of the hill field keeping an eye on all who pass them.'

That lane took us up onto higher ground and sure enough,

standing at one side of the gate into the hill field were two men. They ushered us through.

The stage was set up in the lower area. We followed one of the Volunteers to where the horses and traps were being tied up and joined the crowds that were gathering. Dad and Terence were sorting out some wooden crates to use as steps up to the stage. I tapped Dad on the back.

'Can I have a word?' I said.

'A word?' Dad replied, turning around. He stood up. 'I wanted to have words with you this morning, but we had to leave early.'

We were moving away from the stage.

'Seán, the stage is unsteady on the right-hand side. Ned needs a hand to sort it out,' Joe called after us.

'We'll have to talk later,' Dad said, turning around and walking back towards the stage.

It was always the same. Everybody else had first call on my father. I watched him steady the planks and walk across them himself to test them.

The man we saw earlier on the bike had been let in after all. There he was talking to Joe, both of them with their heads down, looking at some paper. I wondered if he had anything to do with the IRB.

Dad waved at them and they both waved back. So, Dad must have known him too. Joe hurried over and took his position on the stage. He waited until the clapping had died down before he started speaking.

'Thank you for your warm welcome. Many a person thinks that I have some cheek, pressing on with this aeraíocht, especially after the British military authorities made it so clear that they were not in favour of its going ahead.'

People below groaned and a few shouted, 'Boo!'

'But it's not every day that we have such a distinguished speaker as Mrs Sheehy Skeffington to address us. In the past, she has done sterling work to promote votes for women. In the present, she is doing Trojan work for Sinn Féin. Of course, you are all familiar with what this dear lady had to endure when her innocent husband was murdered by the British in 1916.'

There were more groans of disapproval from the crowd.

'We regret that her reception yesterday was marred by a baton charge and we all come here today with hope in our Irish hearts that the occasion will be vastly different. So, it's my great pleasure to welcome Mrs Sheehy Skeffington.'

The crowd cheered and kept clapping until their hands were sore.

'My fellow Irishmen and Irishwomen,' she began. 'I haven't had as healthy a colour in my cheeks this long time. I must admit it has been heightened by the run from the British military over your lovely hills and valleys.'

More cheers and clapping filled the air.

'This morning, we have gathered to take part in this illegal assembly: Sinn Féin supporters, Volunteers, Cumann na mBan members and a distinguished American reporter, all fit enough to run from the military hounds.'

The audience clapped and clapped and clapped.

'Our visiting reporter may have witnessed a baton charge in Castlepollard yesterday, but England cannot baton a whole nation. We will pursue our demands for an Irish Republic and we will not sell our birthright for anything less.'

Mrs Sheehy Skeffington went on to talk about the disgrace of the war in Europe, about the millions who were killed, thousands of Irishmen among them. The Cuman na mBan women were all in uniform, standing on one side of the stage. I spotted Madge Maguire among them. She watched Mrs Sheehy Skeffington as if she were a holy apparition.

Miss Malone, wearing a dark green hat, was perched on a stool behind Mrs Sheehy Skeffington. A pencil in her hand moved furiously as she scribbled notes into a little notebook. The mystery man we had seen with the bicycle sat beside her. His hands were in the pockets of his overcoat and he had his peaked cap pulled down to shade his eyes. It reminded me of Malachy's cap on the day of the raid. The stranger leaned over and said something into Miss Malone's ear. Whatever he said surprised her and she put her hand up to her mouth to stop herself from laughing.

Three Irish dancers came up and took their positions soon after. I stood at the back of the stage, fiddle at the ready. Mrs McGolderick, the Irish dance teacher, gave me the nod and I played the opening bars of 'The Crock of Gold'. The girls all pointed their toes and took off on the right note. Between all the hornpipes, reels and jigs that followed, I searched the crowd for Alice. I even thought I saw her coming towards the stage after the six-hand reel. But when the black-haired girl came closer, she was taller and thinner than Alice. When it came to the time for the dancers to take a break, I climbed down from the stage. Miss Malone kept clapping her hands, even though everyone else had stopped.

'Young man, you are one talented fiddle player,' she said. 'I want you to meet somebody.' She pulled me over to a man in a brown suit and soft brown hat. He was standing with his hands in his pockets.

'Jasper, this is Colm Conneely, the boy I met last night.'

The man took my hand and shook it.

'Nice playing. You're the kid we missed in Kells?'

'I am,' I answered.

'I liked your playing. The crowd liked your playing. You got a quality that grabs people's attention. You fourteen?'

'Yes, on Tuesday.'

Somebody called me and said it was time for a slow air.

'You gotta go,' said Mr Delaney. I stepped on the crates up

onto the stage and played the opening notes of 'The Cualann'. The talking in the crowd shrank to a few whispers and then to that hush that comes over people when they're listening and almost feeling the tune, like I was, with my fingers and my bow. Even the man in the tan overcoat, who had been whispering to Miss Malone earlier on, stopped talking to Joe when I started to play.

I finished on a soft note. Joe Kennedy put his fist up in the air at the good job I'd done. The applause from the crowd rang through the hills. As I was climbing down from the stage, somebody tapped my shoulder.

'How are you about other musicians?' asked Miss Malone.

'Pardon?' I said.

'About *playing* with other musicians?' said Mr Delaney. 'Have you done much of that?'

'I've played at concerts, feises and aeraíochts with other people … lots of times.'

'And your health's good?' he asked.

'Yes.'

'And you've never been in trouble with the law?' he asked.

'Don't answer that question. He's just kidding,' said Miss Malone. 'Look, I know I told you all the jobs were filled…'

'But we could make one more spot,' said Mr Delaney. 'Wouldn't you love to go to the States? I'm sure your folks would like you to grab this opportunity.'

I paused for a second. He was offering me a job. Passage to America, job in America, playing music in America. And Dad knew how much this would mean to me.

'I'm sure they would.'

'Seán's your Dad, right? We could talk to him when the show's over,' said Miss Malone.

'Thanks, but *I'll* talk to him first if you don't mind.'

'We'll be in the Greville Arms Hotel in Mullingar for the next two nights,' said Mr Delaney. 'On Tuesday, we're heading to Dublin. It's over to Liverpool from there and then back to the States.'

'Thanks to both of you for the—'

'Colm, if you want to go, and once your old man is happy to let you go, you're in,' said Miss Malone. 'Why not come to Mullingar tomorrow, and we'll talk?'

She took off unsteadily in her shiny black shoes through the rough grass, Mr Delaney leading the way. I felt like jumping up on the stage and announcing to the world that I, Colm Patrick Conneely, was going to America. A madcap notion, I know, but what do you do when the very thing that you wanted most in the world was snatched from you, only to be given back when you were least expecting it?

Telling Dad about it had to be done carefully. As if he knew what I was thinking, he appeared before me. And 'happy' wasn't a word I'd use to describe my 'old man'. It was time to talk.

Chapter Twenty-Four

'I was talking to Terence last night and he had a very strange tale to tell me,' Dad said.

'About the British soldier?' I said.

He stopped.

'How did you know?'

'I was awake when you were coming to bed.'

'You were listening?' he asked.

'I couldn't help it. You woke me up.'

'First of all, I want to know what you were doing under the platform. I sent a message that you were to go straight to Tom Cooke's.'

'I didn't get the message in time. I couldn't see what was happening over at the bank, so I moved forward.'

'I thought you'd have more sense than that — and to go under the stage?'

'Tom Cooke made me go in there.'

'And why didn't *you* tell me what happened.'

'*Why*? When on earth could I have told you?'

'Last night.'

'I could have if we were on our own.'

'What's that supposed to mean?'

'It means you have time for everybody else, but when it comes to—'

'Pah,' said Dad, waving his hand. 'All in your own mind. For God's sake, tell me what happened.'

'There's hardly anything to tell. Terence was making a story out of nothing.'

'So, you didn't talk to a British soldier or give him anything or shake hands with him?'

'I did all of those things, but not in the way Terence said.'

'What do you mean, Colm? You're not making sense.'

'Look, remember that soldier in Norwood House?'

'What has he to do with it?'

'He was the man under the platform. When I saw him in the house, he was having some sort of fit. He thought I was German, or at least he asked me if I was German or French. He saw me take the gun and I convinced him it was for a sergeant downstairs.'

'I thought you told me—'

'Let me finish. Something strange was happening to him. He thought he was back in the war. Grabbed my leg and really hurt me too. He asked about Miss Fernsby, who must be his aunt, and I said she was downstairs with the sergeant.'

'And you told us all some cock-and-bull story.'

'I admit I did. But when the stones banged on the stage yesterday, it seemed to bring on that fit again. This time, he took a hold of my arm and told me he was scared to "go over the top". He thought we were both soldiers in the trenches.'

'Then what did you give him?'

'I remember one of the lads saying that a whistle was blown to tell the soldiers it was time to move up out of the trenches, so I gave him a policeman's whistle I had in my pocket.'

'Policeman's? Where did that come from?'

'I stole it from Kilcoyne's pocket that day I took the police file about you.'

'And what was the idea of giving it to him?'

'Nobody else could blow it once he had it. I was trying to calm him down.'

'You shouldn't have given him anything. People were watching. Terence saw it all.'

'That soldier held onto my arm and wouldn't let me go,' I said louder. 'He was hurting me. What if he killed me?'

'For God's sake, keep your voice down and stop that foolish talk.'

Nothing was said for a few seconds. Then Dad stepped closer and whispered, 'And what was the idea of shaking hands with him?'

Was he ever going to give up about Terence's story?

'*He* shook hands with me, that's why. I had no choice! Why is it that you're always ready to believe Terence McKay?' I shouted at him.

'Maybe because he doesn't make stories up!' he shouted back at me. He started to walk away.

People were watching us, Lizzie Scarlett among them. She looked like she was trying to decide whether or not to come over to me. Others were drawn to us once they heard Irish being used in a row. One man in the Gaelic League moved closer, trying to make out what we were saying. Dad nearly knocked him over when he was storming off.

One thing for sure, this was not the time or place to raise the subject of going to America. I'd have to wait until I saw him at home.

A mist was coming down over the hills. I trudged through the mud back towards the area in front of the stage. There was Terence, in a lively chat with somebody. I couldn't make out who it was at first, but as I came closer, I could see it was Alice. She was laughing so hard her shoulders were shaking. I turned around and went the opposite way. Neither of them was going to see my red angry face. I waited until I saw Alice climb up onto the stage.

She played a slow air on the tin whistle. Her eyes were closed. Her hair was in a plait brought to the front over one shoulder and tied with a red velvet ribbon at the end. The tune was sad but very sweet. I didn't catch the name of it, but it reminded me of one of Nan's *sean-nós* songs from Connemara. As she played, the red ribbon loosened and dropped onto the stage and her plait started to unravel. I watched it and wondered what it would be like to touch her hair.

Towards the end of the tune, a little white terrier strayed into the crowd and started howling along with the whistle. Joe came up onto the stage.

'We'll have to commend both Miss Alice McCluskey, the Belfast girl, and Carlow, the Irish terrier. She played a fine slow air from Donegal on her whistle and he sang the accompaniment like the true little Irish patriot he is.' Everyone clapped and laughed.

Some boys and girls recited poems in Irish. The prizes were supposed to be presented after that, but a man's voice called out that the RIC had been spotted on the road, and the presentation would have to take place another day. Joe summoned the Glenidan Fife and Drum Band to play the final tune. When they were standing on the stage, Jack O'Sheehan joined them.

'Come on, all you Rainbow Chasers! Let's finish with "A Soldier's Song".' His fine tenor voice rang out on the hillside and we all joined in.

I slipped through the people standing in front of the stage so that I could stand close to Alice. She turned sideways to face me and smiled. I noticed her hair was back in its plait over her shoulder. I took my place beside her and we both joined in, singing with gusto. Her little finger and mine touched as we stood side by side. We cheered after the final note.

'I saw you talking to those Americans earlier,' she said when the cheering was over. 'Is the man with Miss Malone a reporter too?'

'No, he works in films,' I said.

Mr Delaney and Miss Malone were sitting on a bench near the stage.

'Sure enough, he has the look of it. Is he here to find people to act in films?' she asked.

'He's on the lookout for people, but not in the way you think,' I said. 'It's musicians he's after, to play music in theatres in America for a film he's made in Ireland.'

'And?'

'I went up to Kells a few weeks ago to play for him. Joe Kennedy brought me up. We had a bit of bad luck on the way and ended up in the barracks instead of the hall and I never got to see him. To tell you the truth, I thought my chances were gone until today.'

'What about today?' she asked.

'They both liked my playing — especially "The Cualann" — and they've offered me a job.'

'You're joking!' she said, laughing. But then she stopped suddenly and stared at me. 'My God, you're serious! Did you tell them about me?' she asked eagerly.

'I didn't, Alice. To be honest, I wasn't talking to them for that long. I could hardly take in what was happening.'

'Do they need tin-whistle players?'

'As far as I know, they've been around the country and have filled all the places.'

'Then how is it that they offered you one today?' she asked.

'They made an extra position for me because they liked my playing.'

'Maybe they'll do the same for me,' said Alice. 'Are they paying your passage?'

'Yes.'

'So, if I got a job, we'd only have to pay passage for wee James,' she said. 'I think I'll go over and ask them.'

As much as I admired Alice's spirit, I felt that this was a step too far.

'I don't think you should.'

'Why not?' she asked.

'It doesn't seem right to me,' I said. 'It looks very forward.'

'That's all very well for you to say. You're in already. That doesn't mean the rest of us shouldn't have a chance as well.'

By gum, was I sorry I'd told her anything!

'If you go over now, they'll think I'm blabbing all over the place about getting the job and they might think twice about bringing me,' I said.

'Ach, they'll not mind at all,' she said. 'The worst that could happen is they'll say "no" to me. I'm away over to have a wee word. I'll not be talked out of it.'

She took off like a bullet down the field. She could be so stubborn! I wanted to stop her, but how could I without looking peevish and begrudging? Why had I told her the truth about the Americans? Had she heard a single word I'd said to try to put her off? God knows what she would say to the pair when she went over. Whatever she said, I only hoped it wouldn't scupper my own chances with them.

Chapter Twenty-Five

'Colm!' Tom bellowed from the stage. 'I need a hand here with the barrels.'

I joined him and we lifted the big wooden barrels onto the cart to return to the bars in Fore. At one point, Tom stopped and put his hand on my arm.

'Easy, easy! The barrels will end up as a pile of toothpicks if you bang them down on the cart like that.'

I mumbled an apology and used less force. Every so often, I sneaked a glance over at Alice. Miss Malone and Mr Delaney were shaking hands with her now. Shaking hands! Maybe I had been all wrong about her being forward and showing me up. It looked like she was being offered a place. We both could travel to America together ... I hoisted the last barrel onto the cart.

Arms folded, she was standing by the stage when I turned around.

'No good,' she said. 'They've got two tin whistle players from Dublin and aren't looking for any others.'

So, it wasn't to be.

'That's too bad, Alice.'

'Aye. Some people have all the luck. You're away to play in theatres in America and I'm away to teach the tin whistle to the two wee Fagan girls in Castlepollard at three o'clock tomorrow.'

Before I had a chance to answer, she turned on her heel and hightailed it down the field to join Mrs Maguire. Talking non-stop, the two of them walked towards the gate. Then they climbed into a trap attached to a little piebald pony. Mrs Maguire gathered the reins and off with the pair of them down the lane, with not as much as a glance back.

Everyone was on the move. Ponies and horses pulling traps, brakes, buggies, broughams and sidecars clip-clopped through the three open gates. A big plough horse pulling the cart full of barrels followed. Within minutes, most of the walkers in the crowd were making their way down through the fields. Meanwhile, the cyclists were weaving in and out of the traffic on the lane.

I joined the Volunteers who were swarming around the various stools, benches and planks of wood that had been used to make the stage. Tom Cooke spotted me and called me over to him.

'Your Dad said he has to look after Mrs Sheehy Skeffington and Jack O'Sheehan and that you're to walk home.'

'Who's looking after the Americans?' I asked.

'Joe has arranged for them to be brought back to Mullingar this evening.'

A light rain was falling as I moseyed through the long grass with my violin case. Peter was walking in the same direction and joined me.

'I've been trying to find you since you finished playing. Can't wait to blow that whistle! Will we head over to the long field now?' he asked. We had planned to cut across the long field and hide behind the wall at Terence's gate to scare the Reillys on their way home.

'I think I saw the Reillys leave early,' I lied. I was too tired to explain. 'We missed the boat today.'

'Never mind,' said Peter. 'We can have fun doing that another time. I saw you talking to Alice McCluskey.'

'That's right.'

'Did she say why she stopped coming to music?'

'No.' I was also too tired and too cross to explain about Alice, and nor was I ready to tell him about the Americans.

As we were passing by Gilsenans' yard, the big galvanised gate opened and out came the mystery man in the tan overcoat, pushing a bicycle. He swung his leg over the bar and pedalled down the road.

'Do you know who that is?' I asked Peter.

'I don't know him, but he must know your father. I spotted the two of them behind the stage yapping away.'

'In English or Irish?' I asked.

'Too far away to hear,' said Peter. 'But you'd know by the pair of them they knew each other.'

We said our goodbyes at the crossroads beyond the village. Hard as they tried, the black clouds in the sky could hold on to their rain no longer and showed no mercy as I tramped along the mucky road. Within twenty minutes, I was that wet, I might have been sitting under the pump in the yard. As I crossed in through the fields to avoid the mud of the boreen, the line of sycamores beside the back gate were never so welcome a sight. Nan was cutting up a loaf of brown bread when I walked into the kitchen.

'Get out of those wet clothes before a morsel goes into your mouth,' she said when she saw my dripping jacket. A few minutes later, I sat at the fireside, a mug of tea in one hand, and a slice of brown bread and gooseberry jam in the other. Nan started with the questions; Dad called this 'the cross-examination'. She'd not sit easy until she had the whole picture in her head.

'There was an American reporter at Tom's,' I said. 'And—'

A loud rap at the door. Nan and I froze. Another louder rap.

'We weren't expecting anyone,' said Nan, pulling the shawl around her shoulders.

'I'll get it,' I said, jumping up. I opened the door slowly. The mystery man stood on the doorstep — tan overcoat, his knapsack on his back and the rain dripping off the peak of his cap.

I heard footsteps behind me and Nan grabbed my arm.

'Hello, Mam,' said the man in front of us.

It was a woman's voice that spoke.

Chapter Twenty-Six

'**M**am?' I repeated.

'Good God, I thought it was a man at the door,' said Nan. 'Come in, come in.'

'Not before I'm properly introduced to my nephew,' said the woman, putting out her hand.

'This is your Auntie Sheila,' said Nan. 'Sheila, this is Colm.'

The famous Auntie Sheila! No wonder she was at ease talking to Dad. And Miss Malone? Maybe she knew her in America.

We shook hands and she came into the kitchen, taking off her tan overcoat as she moved towards the hearth. She spread it over the back of two chairs in front of the fire and sat in Nan's chair to pull her boots off.

'It's a pity you didn't send us a bit of notice, instead of arriving like a thief in the night.' Nan looked at Sheila's trousers. 'And, I might add, dressed like one, too.'

'Believe me, when you're travelling alone on a bike, it's easier like this,' she said, pinching her trousers, 'and safer. When I go by train or by tram, I wear my proper woman's attire,' she said and winked at me. 'By the way, I managed to get a hold of Seán today. We had a good chat at the aeraíocht. He's staying in

Tom Cooke's tonight. He'll be back in the morning.'

Dad's reaction to my story about the British soldier had rattled me today, but he was still the first person I wanted to tell about the job in America; the first person after Alice, that is. That news would have to wait until the morning.

'Don't worry, I'm changing into dry clothes,' she said when she saw Nan scowling at her wet shirt and trousers. 'Does she hound you over damp clothes?' Auntie Sheila asked me, smiling. I said she did.

Then she slipped into the parlour to change, after throwing her laced-up leather boots sideways beside the basket of turf. Nan put them standing upright and moved one of her crochet cushions onto the chair closest to the hearth. She went around the kitchen, straightening some of the cups on the dresser, sweeping any dirt from the fire that had strayed further than the hearth. She never spoke a word.

Minutes later, Auntie Sheila crossed the kitchen in thick woollen stockings. She eased her way onto the cushion and started drying her long, red curly hair with a towel Nan had left out for her. I noticed that she had the same pointy nose as Dad and myself. She was still wearing trousers and a crinkled white shirt.

'To think it's the first time we've met since, since … Colm was a baby,' Auntie Sheila said.

'Don't the years fly by?' said Nan. 'You weren't one to put

pen to paper,' She picked up her knitting. As soon as she had it in her hands, though, she put it back onto the window-sill.

'Are you still doing the cures?' asked Sheila. 'I have corns on my feet that are killing me.'

'I have the right ointment for those,' said Nan, heading into her bedroom to get it.

Sheila turned to me.

'I'm sorry I didn't get to talk to you earlier,' she said. 'There were so many matters to attend to, I thought it'd be better to have a chat back here.'

She looked over at the bedroom door.

'I'm finding it hard to look at my mother with white hair. The last time I saw her, it was red,' she whispered. I told her that I could remember when it was red, too. But I had things on my mind other than Nan's hair, so I changed the subject.

'What's it like to live in New York?' I asked.

She stopped rubbing her hair with the towel.

'New York? I believe it's a great place,' she said. I was hoping for more information than that and was about to ask her another question, but she got in first.

'How is school going, Colm?'

'I finished this week. It went well enough.'

'Finished already? And what are you going to do—'

Nan arrived back holding a small jar.

'Here's the ointment, Sheila. Rub it into your feet every

night before you go to bed.'

She thanked Nan and popped the jar into her knapsack.

'I was just asking Colm about finishing school. So, what's next? Are you staying here on the farm?'

'If I could, I'd love to go to America,' I said. I stopped myself telling her about the job.

'America. Do you hear that, Mam?'

'I do, but nothing's settled yet,' said Nan. 'It's only a notion he has at the moment. And what about you? What brings you to these parts?' Her voice sounded strange, like she was saying lines in a play instead of being herself.

'Me? Officially I'm a Gaelic League teacher. Unofficially, I work for Cumann na mBan,' Sheila said. She stopped as if she wondered whether it was safe to continue.

'Oh, you needn't mind Colm,' said Nan. 'He's well used to hearing things that he has to keep to himself.'

'You work for Cumann na mBan in New York?' I asked.

'No, in Ireland. I've never been to America.'

This was very confusing. Didn't the RIC paper refer to a sister in New York? They must have made a mistake.

'I've been in the area for the last few days, mostly in Castle-pollard.'

'And you didn't think of coming to stay with us?' asked Nan.

'It was handier to stay with Lizzie Scarlett when I was meeting the girls from the local Cumann na mBan branches.'

'What do you do at those meetings?' I asked her.

'Everything from field dressings to transporting arms and ammunition,' she said, rubbing her hair with the towel. 'There's also fundraising, visiting prisoners and even advising people how to avoid contact with the RIC.'

'Bridie Leonard over in Delvin said some of the Cumann girls knit socks for the lads on the run,' said Nan.

'Oh, God help them if they're depending on me for knitting,' said Sheila, laughing as she draped the damp towel over the seat of the chair near the fire. Her face became serious when she turned around again. 'We *do* try to work closely with the local Volunteers, providing intelligence and the likes. I've worked with some of those women over in Delvin and I can assure you they're doing a lot more than knitting.'

Nan sniffed. She wasn't used to being put in her place.

'There you are,' she said, taking up her own knitting and clicking the needles as if she was tut-tutting at Auntie Sheila's thoughts about the Delvin women.

Chapter Twenty-Seven

Auntie Sheila sipped from her cup of tea.

'You did some mighty playing today. Isn't it great to see the fiddle continue in the family?' This last sentence was said to Nan.

'Surely,' said Nan.

'Do *you* play the fiddle?' I asked.

'No, button accordion. That's a fine instrument you have, too, and I'm sure it cost a pretty penny. Is it new?'

'I got it for my birthday when I turned thirteen,' I said. 'It—'

'How long are you staying?' interrupted Nan. She had put away her knitting again and was folding pillowcases, pressing them flat with her hands and patting them.

'Wait, let me talk to Colm. You got the fiddle when you were thirteen? That was a lovely present to get. And you go to Malachy McSorley for lessons?'

'That's right. Do you know him?'

'I've had some dealings with him — through my work.'

I wondered had she heard about the raid on Norwood House. We sat quietly for a moment until Nan spoke again.

'How long are you staying?'

'I'm off tomorrow morning. Michael Collins is in Granard

at the moment, and I was given dispatches this afternoon that I have to get to him.'

Michael Collins! I was going to tell her Dad was with him last year, but something stopped me. It was the way Dad had been so definite about not talking about it. But that wouldn't stop me asking Sheila a few questions.

'What's he like?' I asked.

'He's a divil to work himself and expects everyone else to be the same,' said Sheila. 'That's why I can't delay in the morning. I've to meet him in the Greville Arms.'

'The Kiernans' hotel?' asked Nan.

Nan and Sheila started talking about one of the Kiernan girls called Kitty. I began to nod off and when the two of them went into Nan's room to fix up a bed for Sheila, I made up the settle bed. They continued to talk inside, the hum of their chatting lulling me to sleep.

I don't know how long I was asleep but I woke up to the sound of voices. They were coming from Nan's room. The friendly tone of the earlier chat was gone.

'What I discuss with my brother has nothing to do with you.' Auntie Sheila's voice was raised.

'I'm entitled to know what is being said about me by my

own flesh and blood,' Nan shouted back at her.

'Concerned about your own flesh and blood now? That makes a nice change from turning your back on them at the time when they needed you most. Is it any wonder I left home when I was fourteen?'

'Oh, no wonder at all! There was no talking to you. All you could think of was yourself.'

'Good job, I did! God help me if I had to depend on the likes of you.'

No words were said for a few minutes. When the talk started up again, it was quieter. I couldn't hear what was being said, except that I heard my name mentioned by Auntie Sheila one time. The voices faded to murmurs and I fell back to sleep.

The cock's crow startled me. With all the fuss about Auntie Sheila's visit, I'd forgotten to close the shutters, and daylight flooded the kitchen. My head ached — I felt it was from the shouting during the night — and the brightness made it worse. I took a cup from the dresser and dipped it into the enamel bucket of spring water on the window-sill. What was in it barely filled my cup, thanks to all the tea-drinking the night before. Cups from last night were still on the table, as well as two slices of rhubarb tart on a plate beside them.

The tan overcoat still hung over the back of the two chairs. I wondered if Auntie Sheila's dispatches were in the pockets. Imagine, I thought, there were messages in our house that

Michael Collins would be reading later on today! What was the harm in having a little peek? Weren't we all working for the love of Ireland?

I put my hand into one of the pockets and felt two envelopes. I pulled them out. Often the messages I had to deliver for the Volunteers were scribbled on pieces of paper and handed to me, but these were proper letters and both had simply 'M.C.' written on the envelopes. I longed to read what was in them.

I thought about *The Valley of the Squinting Windows*. There had been an unmerciful fuss about that book last year in Delvin. I wasn't allowed read it, but I had heard that a woman in the book used to steam the letters open in the post office, read what was inside them and seal them again. Would I dare to be so bold? Last night when I was going to bed, the kettle was empty, and now there was only a drop of water left in the bucket on the window-sill. I'd have to go out to the pump for water. Too risky. I decided to put both letters back into the first pocket, and then check the other one.

Apart from two shillings and a box of matches, I could feel an envelope here, and from the ripped paper on the top, I knew it was open. I pulled it out. It was addressed to Sheila at some street in Dublin and I could see from the stamps that it came from America. It was only a letter to Auntie Sheila. What would be the harm in reading it? There could be something interesting about the cause in there.

Dear Sheila,

I hope all is well with you. Thanks for the card at
Christmas and the knitted caps you sent over for
Michael and Joe. I take it that you bullied some poor
girl in Cumann na mBan to make them as I remember
knitting wasn't your forte! We had such a severe winter,
the kids were very glad of them.

Mike has been promoted to foreman in the building
and I'm still working away as a housekeeper. As
you can see from the address, we've moved to a new
apartment. It's got two bedrooms, so the lads are
delighted to have a room of their own finally.

I hope all is well with you and that you're not taking
any foolish risks with that work of yours. I'm waiting to
hear that you have fallen in love with some handsome
Volunteer, so don't disappoint me!

My main reason for writing to you has to do with
Colm. I find myself often wondering about him and how
he is doing. I wrote to Seán once last year and sent him
some money for Colm, but he never answered my letter.
That has made me fret no end, I can tell you. Therefore,

I have a huge favour to ask of you. Could you go and visit them in Glenidan and let me know how things are with him? I know it means seeing Mam again, but you've a kind heart, Sheila, and this would mean the world to me.

The one thing Seán promised me was that he would tell Colm the truth when the time was right. I want to know if he's done that and, if so, maybe I could write to Colm.

I will look forward to hearing from you.

Your loving sister,

Winnie

My mouth went dry. I read through the letter a second time and quickly put it back into the pocket. A blind stranger was discussing me. I could feel my stomach tighten the way it did when Terence McKay used to taunt me in school. I took another sip of water and climbed back into bed. I had only ever heard of one aunt and that was Sheila. Who on earth was Winnie? Why was I never told about her? Why was she so concerned about me? Why was she sending money for me? What was Dad going to tell me when the time was right?

I got back into bed and stared at the table. The flowers on the oilcloth seemed to move in circles like one of those kaleidoscopes you'd buy at a fair. The questions continued to nag at me — question after question, with no answers, around in my head like 'round the house' at a céilí. My eyelids drooped. I felt exhausted. Soon I drifted back to sleep.

I dreamed somebody was knocking at the door. Auntie Sheila went to answer it. With the partition in the way, I couldn't see who was there.

'You've brought the messages?' said a man's voice in what I recognised as Munster Irish.

'I have, Mr Collins,' said Auntie Sheila. I could hear some shuffling of papers. Michael Collins at our house?

'And what about that other letter?'

There was the sound of papers rustling followed by silence.

'This is from your sister, Winnie?' he asked.

'That's right,' said Auntie Sheila.

'She's very concerned about some boy called Colm,' said Michael Collins.

'That's me!' I shouted from my bed, but neither of them seemed to hear me. They continued as if I hadn't spoken.

'All those questions. Why is she so interested in him?' asked Michael Collins.

In my dream, I leaned forward to hear Auntie Sheila's answer. I was finally going to find out what the letter meant! I hardly dared to breathe, I was so intent upon hearing what she had to say. But all that I heard were muffled whispers.

'Oh, that explains it, surely,' said Michael Collins. 'Have to be on my way, Miss Conneely. Thanks again.' The door slammed shut and woke me up. I sat up and saw that Sheila was putting on her coat to leave. Nan was still in her bedroom.

'You're awake,' said Sheila, leaning down to talk quietly. She was wearing the tan coat. Her hair was in a bun and she had her cap in her hand. 'I've to say my goodbyes to you now.'

'Before you go, will you tell me this: who is Winnie?' I asked.

'Winnie?' she said, standing up straight and looking away. She put her cap on, checking that her hair was all underneath. Nan came into the kitchen.

'Colm wants to know who Winnie is,' said Auntie Sheila to her. 'How would you answer that, Mam?'

'I think it's better to wait—'

Auntie Sheila continued, ignoring her.

'Winnie is … one of our own. She was cruelly shut out of this family many years ago.'

'Not now, Sheila,' said Nan, coming towards her. But Auntie Sheila held her hand up.

'Let me speak. He's entitled to know.' She turned to me. 'She's one of our own and it's high time she was treated that way.'

After saying this, she turned around, lifted her knapsack from the chair in the corner and left.

Chapter Twenty-Eight

Nan followed her to the yard and didn't come back. I heard the banging of buckets soon after and reckoned she must have started the milking. Drifting in and out of sleep, I was finally woken by Roddy's barking.

'Stop all that giving out, Roddy!' shouted a voice. The postman had wheeled into the yard on his bike. I pulled on my trousers and stumbled over to the door.

'Two letters this morning, Colm.'

He fished them out of his bag and handed them to me.

'Are you all right?' he asked. 'You're not your usual self.'

'I'm ... I'm all right, thanks,' I said and closed the door. Not my usual self — if he only knew. Within minutes, the same old routine I did every morning had begun: fold up the blankets, put away the settle bed and hang the kettle on the crane. I sat on my usual chair. Pushing some cups out of the way, I rested my arms on the oilcloth and laid my aching head down. It was all the same but I felt different. The words of the letter crowded my brain.

I find myself often wondering about Colm and how he is doing.

The rattling of the latch brought me back to where I was. Nan bustled into the kitchen. I could hear her place the crock of milk on the dresser and take the kettle off the fire. Next, I heard her footsteps making their way towards me.

'You're not feeling well,' she said quietly. 'Will I get you something?'

'No, thanks,' I said, without lifting my head.

Nan drew in her breath and sighed.

'And Sheila's gone,' she said. 'God knows when I'll see her again.'

I could hear that 'won't you feel sorry for me' tone in her voice, but it wasn't going to work today.

'Whatever happened between the two of you that you didn't talk for years?' I asked, lifting my head up from the table.

She shrugged her shoulders and started fixing the cushion on her chair. Roddy began barking outside. Nan looked out the window.

'I wish that dog wouldn't bark at every jackdaw crossing the yard,' she said.

'I heard you arguing during the night. What was that about?'

Shrugging her shoulders again, she opened her mouth to start saying something but shut it twice as fast.

'At least I know who Sheila is,' I said. 'Now will you talk to me about Winnie?'

Roddy was barking again. Nan pressed her lips together and looked out the window.

'There's your father coming in now. He's the one to

talk to you,' she said.

Dad came in. His bloodshot eyes looked uneasily over at me. His skin looked ashen.

'You're very pale. Are you feeling all right?' he said to me.

'A bit of a headache,' I said. 'Nan said you were going to talk to me?'

She stood in front of her chair and put her hands up as if she was surrendering to Dad whatever had to be said. Then she made her way towards her bedroom.

'Where are you going?' Dad asked.

'Into my room to say a few prayers. Have your talk, the pair of you. There's no need for me to stay.'

'If you don't mind, I'd prefer if you *did* stay,' said Dad.

This was something new. Dad usually let Nan have her own way. She sighed and, with a little toss of the head, turned around and sat with an angry plop into her chair. Dad waited until she was settled. He pulled his jumper over his head and threw it at the back of the chair.

'I told you I had something important to tell you when you reached the age of fourteen,' he said.

So here was the famous talk — the longed-for, dreamed-about talk! I nearly laughed when I thought about all the times I'd tried to have it in the past and here he was this morning, straight in. But wait, what did joining the Volunteers have to do with that letter?

'Isn't it to do with the Volunteers?' I asked.

'It isn't.' He held his head in his hands. 'To tell you the truth, I've been dreading this — dreading it for months. God help me, I don't even know where to begin.'

'You could start by telling me about Winnie,' I said.

'How did you find out about her? Sheila swore she didn't say a word.'

'She didn't. I checked her pockets. I was curious about messages for Michael Collins. There was a letter from someone called Winnie, full of questions about me.'

Dad stood up and walked across the kitchen.

'It's fierce warm in here.' He opened the door into the yard. But before he sat down, he looked over at me.

'She's my sister,' he said.

'The sister in New York?' I asked, but I already knew the answer.'

'That's right. I know you read that in the police file and I wasn't one bit happy about it. I thought it would force me into telling you all of this ahead of time.'

'And you let me believe that it was Sheila.'

'Because I was waiting to talk to you.'

'I can't believe that I've never heard of her.'

'It's very hard to explain to ... someone so young.'

'Someone so young,' I repeated. 'But when it suits the pair of you, I'm called "the man of the house".'

'It isn't the same thing,' said Nan. 'Let your father talk.'

'Winnie was the second youngest in our family,' continued Dad. 'Herself and Sheila were great pals growing up. They were a good bit younger than the rest of us.'

'What age is she now?' I said.

'Eh, let's see, she'd be thirty-two now.'

'She was a good girl at home, a great little worker,' interrupted Nan.

'She was also a lovely fiddle player,' said Dad.

Fiddle player? I was about to ask a question, but Nan jumped in ahead of me.

'My only regret is letting her into the city. That was her downfall,' said Nan. 'One of my nieces had started working in Galway and, of course, nothing would do Winnie only to go herself.'

Roddy nudged Dad's knee, forcing him to scratch his white-tipped ear and pat his head. Dad continued, his gaze fixed on the table.

'Fifteen years ago, she started working as a maid in the Great Southern Hotel. She was a pretty, lively girl and had plenty of what we call "followers". That was all very well, but ... she ended up in the family way and had to go into a Magdalen Asylum.'

'Magdalen Asylum?'

'A place where unmarried mothers go to have their babies,'

he said, still not looking at me.

'How long did she stay there?'

'For six months. She left about seven weeks after you were born.'

'So, I was born there?'

'Yes.'

The clock ticked the seconds on the kitchen mantelpiece.

'And what about my mother? — I don't know what to call her now. What about Delia? Was she some woman that you made up?'

'Good God, no,' said Dad. 'Everything I told you about her is true.'

'Except that she wasn't my mother,' I said.

'Look, Colm, Delia and I were married three years at the time and it didn't look like we were going to have any children. We said we'd take Winnie's baby and rear it.'

'You'd take Winnie's baby,' I repeated, trying to make sense of it all.

'We had some money saved up. We gave it to Winnie to go to America to start a new life.'

'She went to America and you took me.'

'That's right,' he said.

'Why was she never mentioned?' I asked. 'You told me lots of stories about growing up and I never heard her name once.'

'Nan and Winnie fell out when she told her the news about,

eh, being in the family way, and Nan said she never wanted her mentioned again.'

'Your own daughter?' I said to Nan.

'You can sit there and say "your own daughter" but she brought shame to our family,' said Nan.

The word *shame* sounded like it had a red line ruled underneath it. I could feel it floating around the kitchen and settling over me.

'So, the woman I thought was my mother wasn't my mother,' I said slowly.

'In a manner of speaking, she *was* your mother. She loved you as if she had you herself.'

'But the mother who had me is alive all this time?'

He nodded. I stood up and walked over to the photograph on the wall. My so-called favourite photograph. The faces of my so-called parents stared out at me as if they were pleased with themselves — almost *congratulating* themselves — on the good job they had made of lying to me.

'I can't believe it. All the prayers at the grave, the masses, the rosaries…'

I turned around. Nan and Dad were both staring at the fire. Roddy looked up at me from the hearth and wagged his tail.

'I never told you this: I used to be jealous of boys in school because they had mothers to go home to.'

'I can see how you'd feel like that, but you have to

understand, we meant well and I was waiting to tell you when I felt you were old enough to hear it.'

'Meant well?' I asked.

'I wanted to wait until you were finished school. If it got out, I didn't want you to be mocked by the other children. Try and see it from my side.'

I surprised myself by laughing. 'Try to see it from your side? You're not the one whose whole life has been a lie.'

A clucking sound came from the far side of the partition. One of the hens had strayed into the kitchen from the yard. Normally one of us would jump up and whoosh it out, but nobody moved. She pecked at some grains on the floor near the dresser. I couldn't care less what she did.

'And you gave out to *me* for making up the story about the soldier in Norwood House.' I paused. I felt like I was a person in the room looking at myself.

'What about the money for the fiddle? Where did that come from?' I asked.

'I can explain about that,' said Dad. 'Winnie sent over some money for you and I thought that was the best way to spend it. As I was saying, she was a gifted fiddle player herself.'

'Then why did you always let me believe that it came from Joe Kennedy?'

He stopped, frowned and shook his head.

'From Joe Kennedy? I don't know what you're talking

about. I swear I'm telling you the truth when I say that.'

Neither of us spoke for a minute.

'And what happened between you and Sheila?' I said to Nan.

'Sheila wanted me to bring Winnie and yourself home. I wouldn't agree … I *couldn't* agree to it and Sheila left. Up and out — said she was going for good.'

'Did you ever try to get her to come back?'

'I did. I wrote to her, I visited her and even asked the local curate to go and talk sense into her, but there was no getting through to that girl,' said Nan.

I knew where she got that from.

'And that letter in her pocket? Winnie has two sons. I always wanted a brother and to think I have two I never knew about. I wonder do they know about me or has the big web of lies spun across the sea?'

Dad stood up, took the poker and prodded a sod of turf that had fallen out of the hearth, pushing it back into the fire.

'At least you were taken care of by someone in the family. I'm your uncle. We share the same blood.'

'Oh, don't start saying "blood is thicker than water". I'm supposed to be grateful for that?'

'I don't know if it's grateful you should be feeling, but—'

'Wait a minute! You're my uncle, not my father. So, who *is* my father?'

'I'm not sure it's my place to tell you.'

'Whose place is it?' I asked.

He got up and walked back to the chair at the table and sat down.

'Please tell me,' I said. 'I've nobody else to ask unless Nan wants to tell me.' She shook her head.

Dad sighed and put his hands on the table.

'This is going to be hard for you to hear,' he said. 'He was a Yorkshire man — an officer in the British Army.'

I waited for the laugh, but none came. Dad looked at me and looked away.

'That made the disgrace even worse,' said Nan. 'An Englishman! It would have been bad enough if the man was one of our own. Thanks be to God your grandfather didn't live to see the day.'

'That must have been a relief all right,' I said, tears stinging my eyes. 'But I wonder what he'd make of this? Lying to me all my life about who I was? The pair of you making up fairy tales about a dead mother and a make-believe father?'

'Seán and Delia saved you from life in an orphanage,' said Nan. 'Is that what you'd have preferred?'

'I'd have preferred to have been told the truth,' I said, wondering why she mentioned orphanages. I always thought they were for children whose parents were both dead. Then the reason dawned on me.

'So, you were going to leave me there? You'd have left me

in an orphanage if they hadn't taken me?'

'There's no point in crying over the maybes and the might-have-beens,' she said. 'I was a poor widow woman hardly able to keep myself, let alone a mother and baby.'

'I don't believe a word you say,' I said, standing up. 'And people coming from all around asking your advice about cures and the like. Why don't you go through your cures … and find one for having no heart?'

'Ah here, there's no need for that,' said Dad.

'That's what you get for all you did for him, Seán. There's gratitude for you now,' she said.

I moved towards the door but stopped and turned back.

'As for you, *Uncle* Seán—'

'Please, Colm, you'll always be like a son to me,' he said.

'But you're no longer like a father to me,' I answered. 'You're one big lie and she—' I said, pointing to Nan. I tried to grasp the right words, but the right words seemed to be beyond me at that moment. I had to get out. Almost tripping over Roddy to get to the door, I crossed the yard and headed for the garden. There's a saying that you can't see the wood for the trees. I climbed my tree but was barely able to see the branches for my tears.

Chapter Twenty-Nine

I swung up onto the first branch and sat, legs dangling, resting my head against the trunk. The small windows of the cottage looked grimly at me from beneath the rusty galvanised roof. Delia and Kit Fitzsimons were nothing to me! All of the new information about myself flashed through my head. It felt like I was learning facts for a test and the test was about me. I was sorry I hadn't more time with Sheila. She might have answered some questions for me.

Tomorrow I was going to be fourteen. To think that I had been expecting to be welcomed into the Volunteers! What would they say if they knew my real father was English and an officer in the British Army? What if he had fought the rebels in Dublin in 1916? He might have fought in France or Belgium. He could be dead now, for all I knew. I never asked his name. Did he know about me? If I joined the Volunteers, I could end up fighting him. He was my father. Seán was my uncle.

Miss Malone's question came back to me: 'Seán's your Dad, right?'

'He's not,' I said out loud in English.

I rested my forehead against the rough ridges of the bark.

And to think 'the old me' had planned on seeking out *that man* to discuss going to America. Mr Delaney's voice rang in my ear: 'Wouldn't you love to go to the States?'

I answered the question. I had to hear the words. 'Yes. In fact, my mother lives in New York.' That would surprise Mr Jasper Delaney.

I closed my eyes, trying to think. My thoughts were caught up in one big tangle, like the time a stray cat got into the kitchen and unravelled one of Nan's precious skeins of wool all over the floor. Confused as I felt about what was going on, one thing I was clear about: I had to get out of this place. I dropped onto the wall and back into the garden. Dad was standing at the door of the house, as I crossed the yard.

'Nan's in a bad way in there,' he said. 'Could you say something to comfort her?'

'Comfort *her*? She's *your* mother. I'm sure you know how to comfort her,' I said, passing by him into the kitchen.

'You're impossible to talk to,' he called after me and headed down to the workshop. Nan was in her bedroom I could hear her praying the rosary. If I went over to the door and knocked, it'd be all about how upset *she* was and how I was the cause of it all. As if I had any say in the matter.

Instead, I crossed the kitchen down to the parlour, got my old knapsack and threw some clothes into it along with an old snuff box stuffed with coins that I had hidden among my books. Malachy's reference that I had for Kells was still on the shelf, so that went in with everything else. Back in the kitchen, I grabbed a mug, filled it with milk from the jug and took one long drink from it. The old china cat on the dresser smirked at me as if to say, 'Now you know!' I grabbed it by the neck and threw it at the wall between the two back windows, inches below the famous wedding photograph.

It smashed into pieces. Part of the head with the painted mouth smiled its last triumph from the floor. I picked it up and threw it into the fire. Then I noticed a rolled-up note, lying among the smithereens. It was my first time ever to see a five-pound note.

'Thank you, Uncle Kit, though you're no longer my uncle,' I said, pocketing the money. I buttered a couple of slices of brown bread and spread some gooseberry jam on them to make a sandwich. That went into my bag along with an enamel mug. Once I had my cap on, I hauled the knapsack onto my back and grabbed my violin case. The clock chimed one o'clock. I lifted the latch of the door, patted Roddy and said 'goodbye' to him in English. To avoid being seen by Mrs Friary, I climbed over the gate into the woods and crossed over the Well Field.

I filled my mug with cold water from the well and sat on the nearby stile, to eat my sandwich. Food in my stomach, thirst quenched, I was ready to face the walk ahead.

Chapter Thirty

I leaned against the stone wall of Fagan's in Chapel Street in Castlepollard. On the other side of the wall, Alice was playing 'Dilín Ó Deamhas' on the tin whistle in the front parlour. I closed my eyes as one of the little children played the tune in fits and starts. Voices spoke, then the front door opened. Alice was fixing a cream-coloured hat on her head. Two black plaits swung down, tied at the end with cream ribbons.

'Colm! I'm glad to see you,' she said in Irish as she closed the door.

'About yesterday—' I said.

'Don't remind me about yesterday,' she said. 'When I think about what I said and did…' she began but stopped when she spotted my knapsack and violin case. 'You're away now?'

'I am,' I said.

'Have you a wee minute to walk me over to Boyhan's? I've to meet Mrs Maguire there and I usually take the shortcut,' she said.

I told her I had. Crossing the road at the schoolhouse, we took the path on one side of the silent classrooms. It didn't seem right to disturb the quietness of the schoolyard, so we walked on, neither of us saying a word. Not until we were in the woods beyond it, did Alice speak.

'Ach, Colm — about yesterday ... there *is* something I want to say. If I got that job, me and wee James'd have gotten to see Ma. I couldn't think straight, to be honest. I miss her so much.'

I was at a loss as to what I should say to this. We walked on quietly for a few minutes.

'You're dead quiet,' she said. 'Something's happened.' She stopped and held my arm.

'Please tell me,' she urged.

'You know the way your mother is in New York,' I said, and started walking again.

'Yes,' said Alice.

'My mother is also in New York.'

'What? But I thought she was dead,' said Alice.

'I was never told about her,' I said. 'There were two different women: one who had me and left for America and one who wanted to raise me but died.'

'Start from the beginning,' she said, and I told her the whole story. The letter, the questions, the conversation with Dad and Nan all poured out.

'I still can't believe it,' I said at the end. She squeezed my arm and stopped. We faced each other and she put her arms around me and hugged me. I brushed my face against her black hair. It smelled of Sunlight soap.

'That was a hard story to tell,' she said.

'So, you can see why I'm off.'

'I can, but I wouldn't be so hard on your Dad and Nan,' she said.

'What do you mean?'

'They thought they were doing the right thing. Look, wasn't your Dad going to tell you? I feel a wee bit sorry for him, to tell you the truth. What did he say when you told him you were away to America?'

'I didn't tell him.'

'Didn't? Ach, Colm! I'm sure he'll be worried sick wondering where you are.'

'Can't think why.'

'Why? Because he cares about you. He'd not be worrying about you if he didn't care about you.'

'What about Terence McKay?' I said. 'The pair of them seem to get on much better than we ever did.'

'Sure, don't you know it wouldn't be the same with him as it is with you,' she said, squeezing my arm again.

'I'm not so sure about that!' I scoffed. 'And when I think of my real father, an Englishman, an officer in the British army — the very people we're trying to get out of the country—'

'We can't help who are our parents are,' said Alice. After a moment she added: 'I never told you my father is in prison in Belfast.'

I didn't tell her that I already knew this.

'He's to join us when he gets out if he ever gets the money together.'

We strolled along the path beneath the beech trees. Our arms brushed off each other and my hand felt for hers. Over the last few weeks, I had often wondered would I ever get the chance to walk hand-in-hand in the fields with Alice. And now here we were. I glanced at her sideways and could see a little smile on her lips. In spite of all that had happened, I couldn't help smiling myself.

To one side, the ditch was overflowing with wild carrot. We climbed the gate into Johnny Boyhan's field. Two red cows were drinking from the water trough near the ditch. Once we passed them, they fell in behind us, curious as to what we were about. Alice kept turning around to see if they were still there.

'I'll never get used to those beasts,' she said. 'I can't be at ease when they're following me like that. That's the worst about being a city girl in the country!'

I let go of her hand and walked behind her. Her two long plaits swung from side to side as she made her way through the grass. I followed her and the two cows followed me. Our little procession made its way over the field towards the gate. Beyond that lay the Boyhans' garden.

As she opened the gate, I gave one of her plaits a little tug. She turned around and I took her two hands and held them.

'I've got to go,' I said. 'Will you write to me, Alice?'

'Have you an address?' she asked. I rooted in the bag for the leaflet and gave it to her.

'You never know, when my mother sends me the passage, we might even meet,' she said, folding the paper and putting it into her pocket. A tear was working its way down her cheek and I took one of the plaits and dried it away with the cream ribbon.

'Wait here a wee minute,' she said and ran into the house. I closed the gate and leaned against it. After a few minutes, she came back out with a few sheets of paper folded in an envelope.

'I asked Mrs Boyhan for this,' she said, pressing it into my hands.

'I'll be able to afford my own paper,' I told her.

'This isn't for you to write to me. It's for Seán. Write him a few wee lines before you leave. Let him know at least that you're all right. Take care.'

'Alice!' Mrs Boyhan put her head out the door.

I slipped the envelope into the knapsack.

Alice stood beside the woodbine in the hedge and I breathed the smell of it in the damp air. Our noses almost touched, but I felt too shy to kiss her on the lips. Instead, I lifted her hand to my own lips. I will never forget the softness and the smell of her skin. She tried to smile, but tears in those black eyelashes were gathering. I watched her turn around and run back into the house.

This was never going to be easy. My mind was ordering me like a sergeant in the army to move away quickly; I had to get on the road. My heart was telling me to linger; leaving was painful and should be given time.

Chapter Thirty-One

The truth was if I was serious about getting to Mullingar, I hadn't any choice. I *had* to get on the road. On I went through the garden to the old elm that everyone called the 'Belly Tree' on account of its swollen trunk stretching over the ditch. There was a gate beside it onto the road. I needed a tune in my head to help me and settled on a slip jig called 'My Mind will Never be Easy'. I let it play away to banish the words of my mother's letter, the sound of Nan praying before I left, and the sight of Alice's tears. I walked along the Dublin road to the rhythm of the tune until the church bell in Castlepollard rang four o'clock. A horse and trap for Float Station would be leaving from Brogan's at twenty past four. I started to walk faster, as fast as I could go with my fiddle and my knapsack.

Bratty Road was up ahead and, coming closer to it, I noticed a Ford car stopped at the top of it. Two policemen stood behind it. Keeping my eyes on the road, I passed them, but a voice shouted at me to stop — the last voice I wanted to hear at that moment. I stood exactly where I was and didn't look back.

'Turn 'round, boy!' said the voice. I turned around and

found myself facing Kilcoyne.

'You're that boy,' he said. 'This young lad was in Glenidan, Constable Harris — the night I searched it with Sommers.'

'Seán Conneely's son?'

'The very one.'

I stood, keeping my gaze on the far ditch. There was no point in denying the fact to this lot.

'What's in that bag of yours?' asked Kilcoyne.

I stood, not saying a word.

'Search him. He could be delivering messages.'

I was going to say that I didn't know it was against the law to deliver messages. Instead, I said nothing and handed the bag to Harris. He rooted through it.

'Doesn't seem to be anything in here but clothes,' he said. Pushing my arm aside, he put his hand into the pocket of my trousers, pulling it out triumphantly.

'Wait a minute. What's this?' He tut-tutted. 'A lad like you with a five-pound note?'

He held up the five-pound note and waved it at Kilcoyne.

'I can explain that,' I said.

'You can *explain*, can you? Off you go explaining then,' said Kilcoyne.

'I broke a statue of a cat at home. It was left to me by my uncle. We didn't know there was a five-pound note in it until it smashed.'

Both men laughed.

'I'm telling you the truth. That's where it came from,' I said.

'Well, I've heard many a tale, but that's got to be the tallest one yet,' said Kilcoyne. 'It doesn't explain to us either, why you were in such a hurry on the road just now.'

'There's a reason for that—' I started.

'Not interested,' said Kilcoyne. 'Better check the violin case too.'

Harris reached over to take it, but I held onto it.

'Hand it over, boy, or you'll be brought to the barracks.'

He tried to prise it out of my hands. I held onto it at first, but then I let it go for fear he'd damage it. He put the case down on the ground, opened it and grabbed my fiddle.

'Ever learn how to play one of these, Constable?' he said holding it up to Kilcoyne.

'Not likely,' said Kilcoyne.

'Could I have it back now, please?' I asked.

'We'll have to think long and hard about that,' said Kilcoyne. 'You might have to wait in the barracks while we consider what's best to do.' He handed the fiddle back to Harris who snapped it back into its case.

'But I—'

'And then there's the matter of the five-pound note,' said Harris. 'I wouldn't be surprised if we heard within the hour of that money being stolen.'

Kilcoyne walked around me as if he was inspecting me. Then he stood in front of me and brought his face up close to mine. I wanted to step back but I was afraid to do anything to spoil my chances of getting away — so I stood there.

'Better still, your father might come to the barracks looking for you,' said Kilcoyne.

'I can't go to the barracks; I've got to be in—'

'Boy, we don't *have* to know nor do we *want* to know where you have to be. Get into the back seat and not another word,' said Harris, opening the door. I climbed in. He handed my fiddle and knapsack to Kilcoyne in the front.

Harris turned the crank to start the car. The engine warmed up. Could I open the door and make a run for it? But I wasn't leaving without my knapsack and fiddle.

Harris climbed in.

'Drive to the barracks, Harris,' said Kilcoyne.

That drive was only a few minutes, but in that time, I could imagine the passengers waiting outside Brogan's Hotel in the Square as the horse and trap pulled up to take them to Float Station.

Once inside the barracks, Kilcoyne pushed me into a room; it had to be the smallest in the building. A few butts of cigarettes lay flattened into the bare floorboards. A narrow wooden bench leaned against one wall. I sat down on the only other piece of furniture in the room — a three-legged stool, with the initials 'C.B.' carved into it. I didn't know what they'd done with my knapsack and fiddle, never mind the five-pound note.

The front door of the barracks opened and banged. A man's big laugh followed. Boots clattered across the flagstones in the hallway outside.

'It was handed in by a woman yesterday,' said a voice.

'More power to her,' said another. 'Did she leave a name?'

'She didn't, Mr McSorley,' said the first voice. I could hear what sounded like a drawer being opened and things being moved around in it.

'One watch returned to its owner.'

I banged at the door.

'Malachy, Malachy!' I shouted.

After a minute, I heard a key unlock the door of the room I was in. The door opened and Malachy McSorley and Sergeant McCarthy stood in the doorway.

'What on earth...?' asked Malachy, looking into the room to see whether anyone else was with me. Kilcoyne appeared in the doorway.

'This young man was searched on the public road and found to have five pounds on his person, along with a cock-and-bull story about how he came to possess it.'

'On what grounds is he being detained?' asked Sergeant McCarthy.

'On the grounds that he has a considerable sum of money on his person for which he cannot give a sensible account and—', but Sergeant McCarthy held up his hand.

'Thank you, Constable Kilcoyne. I'd have to say that I'm uncomfortable detaining a young person based on such evidence. I'd feel much happier questioning him myself.'

'But we—' objected Kilcoyne.

'As I said, Constable, I'll take it from here.'

The policeman stood in the doorway.

'Yes, sir,' he said, barely opening his lips, and the face on him! You'd swear he'd taken a bite out of one of Nan's crab apples. He turned around and left. Malachy was about to follow him, but the sergeant patted him on the shoulder.

'Would you mind staying with me, Mr McSorley?' asked Sergeant McCarthy.

'Of course, Sergeant.'

He shut the door and Sergeant McCarthy sat down on the bench. Malachy squeezed in beside him.

'Sit down there, young Conneely,' said the sergeant, nodding in the direction of the stool. 'Start at the beginning. And I want the truth, please.'

Chapter Thirty-Two

The truth. That word had a different meaning for me now. One thing for certain, I wasn't going to let 'the truth' stand in my way. Nor had I any intention of starting at the beginning. I told the two men that I had knocked the cat off the dresser shelf by accident. I also led them to believe that Dad and Nan knew that I had the five pounds.

'I can see how the constables thought it was made up,' said the sergeant. 'But remembering that uncle of yours, I for one believe you.'

I felt like screaming: 'He's Delia's brother. He's not my uncle!' but said nothing.

'That was Kit Fitzimons all over,' said Malachy. 'Very careful with the money and not inclined to part with it. Well, I'm happy to vouch for this young man, once he tells us where he was going with the five pounds.'

I knew there was no way out of answering this question.

'Remember Jasper Delaney and the fiddle players he was looking for?' I said.

'I do indeed. What? You got an offer?'

'I did, for all the good it is to me now. Thanks to ending up here, I missed the lift to Float Station this evening. The Yanks are leaving Mullingar for Dublin in the morning.'

'Wait here a minute.' Sergeant McCarthy slipped out of the room.

'I'm surprised your Dad didn't come as far as Castlepollard to see you off,' said Malachy, once we were on our own.

'He wanted to avoid the RIC,' I said, feeling my cheeks burn. There were many safe places he could have said goodbye to me in Castlepollard.

Sergeant McCarthy bustled in. After placing my knapsack and violin case on the floor inside the door, he handed me the five-pound note.

'I've checked with the men inside. Nobody's going to Mullingar tonight, but there'll be a truck leaving early in the morning. You could go in with it as far as the station.'

It didn't feel right travelling with the enemy, but what choice had I?

'Thanks,' I said.

'And there's an empty cell across the hallway there, if you want to bed down for the night.'

I was going to refuse and go to Joe Kennedy's. Then I thought of all the questions I'd be faced with and thought better of it.

'Thank you, Sergeant.'

'Good luck, Colm,' said Malachy. He stopped at the door. 'I'll look forward to hearing how you're getting on.'

The bang of the front door closing shook the walls. I went into the cell. The sergeant disappeared into another room and came back with a mug of soup, and a blanket over one arm.

'I've let the others know you're here and they'll give you a shout in the morning. I was thinking you must be hungry. There's something from the kitchen to keep you going.' I took the mug of soup. It smelled of onions, potatoes and the parsley that was floating on the top. 'And here's a clean blanket.' Clean the blanket may have been, but the cell stank of Jeyes Fluid.

The evening sun shone through a little square window, too high for me to look out, even if I stood up on the stool beneath it. After I'd drained the mug of the last drop of soup, I stretched out on top of the blanket. Whatever it was made from made me itch. I thought about motoring to the station in the morning. Would any of the Volunteers see me going off in a chariot? What would they think? Did it matter now?

'He'll be worried sick wondering where you are,' Alice had said about Seán, the man I'd always called 'Dad'. How could he be worried when he'd lied to me all these years? I had always thought of him as my father, the bravest man I ever knew. Yet he hadn't the courage to tell me the truth about myself, or the truth about his own story either. Memories of being minded by him as a little boy in the fields came back to me as I lay on that wooden bed; and the way he used to play hide-and-seek with me in the barn and read stories to me at night by the fire.

'He was like a mother and father to me,' I said out loud as I punched the wall with my fists. I lay back on the slab, my knuckles throbbing, and closed my eyes.

Outside, two girls were arguing about whose turn it was to hold a skipping rope. A mother shouted down to them from a nearby house and I could hear the skipping rope being turned again. It was to the rhythm of 'The Waves of Tory' and, in spite of the smells and the scratchy blanket, I drifted off to sleep.

I don't know what time it was when I was jolted by three loud bangs on the knocker of the barracks door. The bolt was pulled back and the door creaked open. I heard voices but I couldn't make out the words. A couple of thumps on my door followed, and Sergeant McCarthy shouted, 'You've a visitor.'

He walked in, cap in one hand and a candle in the other.

I sat up and tried to focus my eyes as he came towards me. His big rough hand patted mine.

'Easy now, son,' he said, putting down the candle on the floor as he sat on the stool. 'I met Malachy on the road. He was on his way to me and I was on my way to Castlepollard. I don't know why, but I had a feeling you might have come this way.'

'It was the letter and being told about—'

'Shh now. It's all right. I was thinking after — the shock it must have been to find out the way you did.'

'I'm sorry I didn't tell you I was going,' I said. 'I was going to write to you. I've paper and an envelope in my bag.'

'Malachy was telling me why you were brought in. To think that ugly cat had a five-pound note up its rear end all these years,' he said, shaking his head.

If he had said this at home, we'd have both laughed and laughed. But I couldn't even bring myself to smile.

'He told me you got offered that job you were after,' he said.

I clenched the blanket. Had he come to try and make me stay?

'I won't deny that we'll be sorry to see you go,' he said, lowering his voice. He looked away for a minute. 'I wouldn't stop you for the world, but if you ever change your mind, you're always welcome home.'

'Thanks,' I said. Home. There was no denying that Glenidan was home to me, regardless of all the lies.

'Where's that sheet of paper you were talking about?'

I pointed over to my knapsack. Once he had the envelope, he pulled out the sheet of paper and placed it on the stool. Kneeling on the floor, he took the red pencil from behind his ear and wrote something down. He folded it and put it back into the knapsack.

'That's your mother's address,' he said. 'I'm going to write and tell her that you know about her and that you're heading over to New York.'

'Thanks,' I said again. I was trying to think of something

else to say when he patted my arm and leaned down to whisper in my ear.

'I'm sorry, son.'

I swallowed and felt tears stinging my eyes.

'They'll never let you leave the—' I started.

'Shh. Never mind me. I'm a hardy divil, don't you know.'

He sat down and a quiet ease settled between us. I started feeling drowsy. The door opened and closed gently. There were voices outside. One voice sounded like it was reading something. Dad's voice answered. I tried to stay awake, but sleep got the better of me.

I dreamt I was walking up the boreen when I met Nan.

'Colm Conneely! Give me back that jumper,' she said, tugging at my sleeve.

'Why?' I asked, pulling away.

'Because it's all wrong. I knitted it for the old Colm, not for you! I'll have to rip that old blue jumper and start a new one. New wool, new pattern, new—' Her voice seemed to shriek the word and I woke up.

Chapter Thirty-Three

What had sounded like the word 'new' now seemed more like 'Yoo hoo' and it wasn't Nan's voice. Light was coming through the little window. The door opened and a head peeped in.

'I had to see if it was you,' a voice whispered. It was Molly McGrath from my class.

'What are you doing here?' I asked.

'This is my new situation,' she said. 'I'm a maid here at the barracks. What are you in for? Mammy always said you'd come to a sorry ending being mixed up with the Volunteers and the likes.'

'I'm not in for anything. I'm only getting a lift to Mullingar station.'

'Shhh. Don't talk so loud, or I'll lose my new situation. You're being transferred to the barracks in Mullingar?'

'No, I'm going to the train station.'

'Are they transferring you to Dublin? Mammy says that's where all the hard cases go.'

'Did they tell you to call me for breakfast?' The smell of rashers and eggs wafted in the door.

'They did. Mammy said—'

'Thanks, Molly. I'll be in for my breakfast in a minute.'

'If you see me in the Day Room, don't talk to me. I don't want to lose my new situation.'

The stub of the candle my late-night visitor had brought in with him the night before was sitting on the stool. Had I imagined it, or had he written my mother's address in New York? I looked around for the sheet of paper. My bag was under the table. I felt inside the top flap and there was the folded sheet, with the address written on it in Dad's scrawl. Underneath he had added the words *Lá breithe sona duit* and there was a ten-shilling note folded into it. My birthday — the day when Winnie Conneely brought me into the world. And here was a note and money from Dad, the man I was so cross with yesterday. Yet he was prepared to come to the barracks, knowing what was going to happen to him, and he did that for me. I put both back into my bag.

My blue jumper caught on a nail in the door on the way out. I cursed the hole it left in the sleeve and the annoying thread dangling from it. Pity I hadn't thought of wearing my good jacket yesterday or even packing it in my bag. Maybe there would be time to buy a new jumper in Dublin. My stomach growled and off I went to follow the smell of the fry.

I saw the words 'Day Room' printed on a door. Looking inside, I saw a policeman sitting at a small table with his pen and ink, writing into a ledger. Kilcoyne and Harris and Sergeant

McCarthy sat on two benches at a long table. Molly was bringing in plates with rashers, eggs and fried bread.

'Sit down there, lad,' said Sergeant McCarthy to me, pointing to the end of the bench. Kilcoyne leaned over and whispered into Harris's ear. They both looked at me as if I had brought an infectious disease to the table.

I kept my head down after that. I was hungry and tucked into the fry. Molly came in with a teapot and filled my cup then hurried back to the kitchen in case I spoke to her.

By the time the clock in the barracks was chiming seven o'clock, I was sitting in the back of a chariot. Harris was behind the wheel. The other man in plain clothes turned around.

'This is the boy Sergeant McCarthy wanted us to deliver to the station?'

'Yes, sir,' said Harris. The first man turned back.

'I believe somebody was brought in last night?'

'Yes, sir, one of the Shinners we've been after. We put him in the cell downstairs.'

'Was he involved in that charade on Sunday?'

'Yes, sir, and other things.' Harris's head tipped slightly in my direction.

'Quite, quite,' said the other man.

They were talking about Dad as if he was some kind of criminal. Did it mean nothing to them that he had risked his freedom to come to visit me last night? I thought of him in the foul-smelling cell, lying beneath a rough blanket.

The road curled through the valley at one end of Lough Derravaragh. Fields stretched down to the lake and I could hear his voice telling the story of the Children of Lir as clearly as if he had been sitting in the back of the chariot beside me. One sister and three brothers changed into swans after their mother died. I used to pity those children not having the likes of Dad and Nan to mind them. That was when I didn't know that my mother was alive. My mother. What did she look like? Was she kind? What did she play on the fiddle? Would she talk to me in Irish? Would she tell me about my father? I needed a tune to keep thoughts of British Officer Father out of my head for the moment. What about 'The Exile's Jig?' I played it in my head and followed it with 'Farewell to Ireland'.

The town was as quiet as the still water of the Royal Canal that we drove alongside. My stomach was feeling a little uneasy from the motion of the chariot, but we weren't far from the station now. A little boy in a ragged coat stood on the path at the Fair Green. He stared at me in the back seat as if to say, 'You couldn't be in worse trouble.' We pulled up outside the station. I said a quick 'thanks' and pulled my knapsack and violin case out of the back seat.

A pony and trap waited close to the main door. The driver, a stout man wearing a tweed cap, shiny with age, watched my every move. The entrance in the corner had two great stone pillars on each side and three steps to the door. I had climbed those steps twice before to travel to Galway.

When I thought about Galway, I thought about Nan. She'd be at home on her own now. I don't know why, but the sight of her on the floor in the parlour beside the broken drum flashed into my mind. That night, I'd been furious with the policeman for being so cruel to Nan. Yesterday, I was raging with *her* for being cruel to my mother — and to me when I was a little baby. Now I was beginning to feel sorry for her, thinking of her all alone in the house. And it wasn't just being alone. I knew she'd be worried about me. Alice's voice came into my head.

'She'd not be worrying about you if she didn't care about you.'

I looked down at the hole in my sleeve and thought about the dream last night. I was starting a new life, but I couldn't just switch out of my old one as if it never happened. Before I crossed the threshold, I decided I'd write Nan a few lines from Dublin. I owed her that much, at least.

Once inside the door of the station, I stood for a minute, wondering if I should wait here for the others. But there was to be no waiting; an American voice drifted from the Refreshment Room.

'I told my editor that one of us needs to get over there and see for ourselves what's going on. He said to me "Jacinta Malone, you're the gal for the job. You're smart, you write a good column and with a name like Malone, you'll blend right in there with all those Paddies".'

'And here you are, Miss.' It was a girl's voice.

I opened the door. The big round Refreshment Room was empty except for six people. Close to the counter sat Miss Malone and Mr Delaney each side of a table covered in a white cloth. Three boys sat with them. They all looked older than me. A maid with a white apron was pouring tea from a shiny silver teapot.

'There he is!' said Miss Malone.

'Hi, kid,' said Mr Delaney, holding up his tea-cup as if to say 'cheers'. 'I need to talk to you.' He beckoned me over to another table. 'We knew you were coming. Joe Kennedy phoned the hotel this morning.'

'Phoned about me?' I said.

'Yeah, he called from the Pollard Arms. Told us you were coming and said to tell you Tom Cooke will look after your grandmother. Some other guy's going to help him—'

'Terence?' I suggested.

'That's him.'

'So, Joe knows about Dad?'

'He most certainly does. "Tell Colm not to worry," he said.

"His grandmother will be in good hands".'

I thought about the day I said to Dad that Terence could look after Nan — trying to take a rise out of him. And now? All I felt was relief.

'You ready to go?' Miss Malone called over to us. Her tongue licked the red lipstick on her upper lip.

We followed her and the other boys out to the platform. Mr Delaney had the tickets. As I stood beside Miss Malone, she looked down at my jumper.

'Honey, we need to get you a new sweater,' she said, pointing to where the nail had ripped my sleeve.

'I had the same thought myself, Miss Malone,' I said, fixing the knapsack on my back.

But truth to tell, at that moment, the ripped jumper was the least of my worries. I, Colm Patrick Conneely, was ready to go. I was on my way.

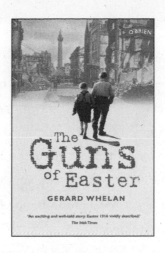

The Guns of Easter

by Gerard Whelan

1916 Rising, World War 1: It is 1916. From the poverty of the Dublin slums Jimmy Conway sees World War 1 as glorious, and loves the British Army for which his father is fighting. But when war comes to his own streets Jimmy's loyalties are divided: his uncle is one of the rebels occupying the General Post Office. Dublin's streets are destroyed, business comes to a halt. In an attempt to find food for his family, Jimmy crosses the city, avoiding the shooting, weaving through the army patrols, hoping to make it home before curfew. But danger threatens at every corner.

A Winter of Spies

by Gerard Whelan

Irish Civil War: A sequel to The Guns of Easter.

This books tells the exciting story of Sarah (Jimmy's young sister) and their family who are involved in the spying activities of Michael Collins during the War of Independence. Sarah, a young eleven-year-old, cannot figure out why her family is so neutral towards the war and why everybody is so secretive. A strong rebel herself, she wants to do her bit for Ireland. Then she finds out the terrible truth - and she too carries secrets which could cost her her life.

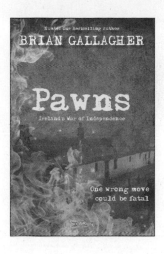

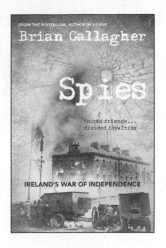

Pawns

by Brian Gallagher

Irish War of Independence: friends Johnny, Stella and Alice grapple with conflicting loyalties – then matters come dramatically to a head on the night the Black and Tans set Balbriggan ablaze during a murderous night of vengeance.

Spies

by Brian Gallagher

Irish War of Independence: as the conflict grows more lethal, the three friends must decide where their loyalties lie. Then a secret from Johnny's past changes everything...